A Mended Heart
beneath These Scars

BASED ON TRUE EVENTS

C. L. HARRIS

Fulton Books, Inc.
Meadville, PA

Published by Fulton Books 2016

ISBN 978-1-63338-306-7 (Paperback)
ISBN 978-1-63338-307-4 (Digital)

Printed in the United States of America

To my husband.
You saved me from so many demons and
the darkness that always tries to arise.
You have been there by my side through
the good times and the bad. I love you, baby.
I can't even imagine my life without you.
Thank you for being my soul mate.

$\mathcal{P}rologue$

When I saw you I fell in love, and you smiled because you knew.
—William Shakespeare

I remember the first day we met because I loved him from that very first day, and I remember how everything around me vanished, leaving only him. How my heart beat so hard it felt like it would pop out of my chest, spilling my soul out for him to see. I remember what he was wearing and the way he smelled, so distinctive that I would know it anywhere. I remember his handsome smile and the sense of security I felt when he was near. Like I was no longer alone in the world, that he would protect me and that my battles were his battles. In many ways on this day, I started toward a destiny I felt I'd never deserved. I met my best friend and my soul mate; my life was changed *forever*.

Whenever I heard "it was love at first sight," I would roll my eyes because to me something like that didn't exist. That was until I met him. I grew up with parents who had a loveless marriage, and my sister was headed down the same path. I never knew what love was, but now I know the real meaning of it, and it is something different all on its own. To me, it means that you just know when you've found the one who shares the same strange feeling in the depths of your soul, and time seems just to stop when he looks at you. The noise fades out, and all that matters is that the beating of your heart and how it seems to match his. In my case, it was love at first sight because I had found the one I was meant to be with. The empty void that was in my heart was filled with his first hello. When we first met, I had no idea how important he would become, that once I saw him there would be no turning back.

When I least expected it, and without explanation, I found someone who understood me as if we've known each other forever; it was as if he was the other half of my soul, and I was his. It's as if we called from the emptiness in our heart looking for that love we desired, and because of this, I am forever his.

CHAPTER 1

The Beginning

New beginnings are often disguised as painful endings.
—Lao Tzu

The day was June 30, 2007, the rain drilled down into the earth. My feet crunched into the desert sand pulling me in, but I just ran faster, trying to leave my past behind me. The only sounds echoing were my heartbeat and the rain. No thought traced my mind as I ran toward an unknown destination. My escape was in the movement of my feet galloping like a stallion. I felt a bead of sweat slide down my temple. My eyes were set on the path before me as I almost reached the end of my run. As I almost reached my goal, I stopped suddenly as some unseen force snapped me back into reality; my ringing cell phone had beckoned me back. As I pulled out my cell phone, I had a sudden strange feeling that I had forgotten something today. But as I searched my mind, I drew up a blank. I answered my phone, trying to catch my breath. The voice of my friend was on the other side of the phone. Then as if I ran into a brick wall, it all came flooding back to me. It was Simone's birthday, and I had forgotten all about her party. I then realized the reason for her call.

"Where are you?" Simone shouted, sounding a little panicked.

"I'm so sorry, I'm late, but I'm on my way now," I replied quickly with sorrow in my voice. I forgot that her party started at two, and it was already 3:30. I stared down at the time on my phone, and I sighed, knowing that my past always had a way of finding me.

As my mom and I pulled up to Simone's house, my mother, Helga, decided to give me another one of her "lectures." I expected this was coming because she always had to find a way to knock me down emotionally, especially when I was happy about something.

"Now, Hailey, you know what the rules are and be on your best behavior…"

Blah, blah, blah. I blocked her out; it got easier every time. My mother always tried to find flaws in me, like how I would never be perfect enough, never smart enough, and how I needed to do something with my life, and hanging out with friends wasn't one of them. This lecture was just the same lecture she always gave me. I knew, however, the rules, and I knew how I was supposed to behave, but she felt the need to always keep telling me that I was not doing good enough. Out of my entire family, I was the only one who behaved; I have stayed clean and out of trouble. I had good grades, and I am the last person she should worry about, but I was caged and leashed and never, ever free. Because of the constant verbal abuse from my mother, I caged my heart. I could never be the real me, and I didn't know if I could ever really trust somebody. My thoughts and my feelings, my mom never approved of. She saw me as a sinner, a burden; and in her own eyes, I was the reason she never had a career, and I'll never be the daughter she wants me to be. She says I will have to answer eventually to God for the sins I have committed and for not treating my mother with more respect. Yet I always loved my mother as a daughter should, but just like everything else, that wasn't enough. She wanted me to follow her every word, to do what she said without thinking about it, to be her puppet. She never saw that the biggest sin that had been committed was her sin against her daughter. The sin where she called her daughter ugly and a basket case; she said and did anything she could to put me down. This started when I was only twelve years old. The greatest sin she committed was when she pushed her daughter so far emotionally that she contemplated ending her life at sixteen.

I remember this day very well; it was the day I realized I needed to free myself from my mother before I was lost forever. I was always a fast learner and had all straight As except for one class, Math. Let's just say math and I were mortal enemies. I was always a step behind, and I worked hard to finally get a grade above a C. I went to show my mom my B because I was proud of myself for working so hard to achieve this grade, yet it wasn't good enough for her. She look me straight in the eye and said, "If you don't get an A, I will divorce your father. Maybe then you will focus on your schooling."

My dad and I had always had a close relationship, and he did his best to protect me from my mother's harshness. I know she said this to hurt me, but it was the last straw. Something inside me gave up, and I just wanted to end the sadness and pain. Logically, I knew that there were others out in the world who go through much worse than me, but after years of being beaten down, I didn't want to do it anymore. However, it wasn't until I was in the shower looking at the razor blade in my hand that I snapped out of it and knew that I was stronger than this and I only had to fight for a little while longer and then I would be free.

The worst part is that she wasn't always like this; I remember there was once a time when she was loving and sweet, when she would stroke my hair because I was sick. But these memories are shattered and replaced with memories that are not kind or sweet.

Locked in my train of thought, a sudden bolt of shock snapped me out as my mother's words registered in my head.

"Hailey Rose Wyatt, are you listening to me?" she screamed, making me cringe; she sounded like nails on a chalkboard. I couldn't stop cringing with every word that left her mouth, and I hated it when she said my name like that.

"Yes, Mom," I replied in a polite tone. No need to get grounded now. Six months ago, I turned sixteen, which meant I had only two more years with her; then… I was free. *Yippee!* My mind screamed as I grabbed my things, and for just a brief moment in my head, I imagined that this day was the day that I left for good. With that amazing thought, I gave myself some false sense of security, even if it was just for the day. I slammed the car door, and a sly smile pulled at my lips. Even if it was just for the day, I thought I would make the most of my day of freedom, and I had a feeling that today something good was headed my way.

I walked up to my friend's front door dressed in my usual tomboyish outfit. Today I was dressed in my green army-printed pants, a slimming army-printed tank top that showed off the curves of my body. I was also wearing my black skate shoes along with an army-printed baseball cap that I wore backward. I added the hat as a last-minute accessory, hoping it would help to hide my still soaking wet hair. I was just grateful as I was standing on Simone's front porch that the rain had finally come to a stop. Living in Tucson, Arizona, it is not long before you realize that the weather can change on the drop of a hat. One day, it could be cold, and by the next, the desert heat would be beating down on your head. However, I was grateful for days like today with it having just rained; the air smelled fresh, and it held a soft chilled breeze. I rang the doorbell and listened as the ringing echoed inside the house, announcing that someone needed to answer the door. The door swung open, and there stood my bouncy and happy friend, Simone.

"I'm sorry I'm late," I greeted her, forgetting to say hello.

"No problem. You're right on time. We were just about to head out to go to Golf 'n' Stuff. By the way, you and Molly are riding in the white Trooper." She pointed at the car, of course as always, with a smile on her face.

"Shotgun!" I shouted as I raced Molly to the assigned car. Molly was a very close friend of Simone's, they met one day in middle school and had been inseparable ever since. When I met them in high school they instantly took me in, protecting me from others and giving me support I didn't get from home. We were all on the soccer team together and had created our own little weird family. Molly was fierce and had such an amazingly big heart. When she found out that our birthdays were only a day apart she made sure that we celebrated it together because it wasn't really celebrated at my house.

As I continue to run to the car I could hear Molly's laugh following behind me.

My warm hand grasped the car door handle, and upon contact, goose bumps crawled up my arm. To me, this was a weird reaction to take place on this humid, wet summer day. I jumped in the car and buckled up, not paying attention to the person who just sat in the driver's seat. Then my attention was pulled to him as he said, "Hello." When I turned to look at him, I was set back by the incredible-looking man. He had dirty brown/blond hair and the most incredible baby-blue eyes I've ever seen. His eyes were the ones you would want to get lost in.

"Hello," I replied, trying not to let my voice shake.

"How you doing, girl?" he rang out in a high-pitched voice.

His vocabulary and posture told me that I was in no way his type. My mouth fell open as he pulled big-framed white female glasses over his perfectly shaped face. Then out of nowhere, he started to laugh and point at me. I became furious. What was so funny about me that gave him the right to laugh? He drew the glasses off his face and threw them onto the back seat.

"I'm so not gay," he blurts out. "I was only testing you."

Testing me? Testing me for what reason? Did I pass? That was all I kept thinking, and I shook the thought from my head. This was no time to start getting paranoid.

"Um, sorry if it wasn't funny. I was trying to see if you were cool or not," he said to break through my space-out.

"Did I pass?" I replied back, trying not to sound like a child asking for approval.

"Yup, you did. I'm Dean, by the way."

"I'm Hailey," I replied, a little too happily and quickly, trying not to pay attention to the fluttering in my chest.

The night went from starting out great to ending stressfully; everything that could go wrong did go wrong. At Golf 'n' Stuff, we were all informed that Molly invited her boyfriend, Allen. This was a foolish thing to do on her part because no one liked him at all, and I mean no one. He was a five-foot, two hundred pounds of angry, rude, and dishonest excuse for a man. On top of all that, he treated Molly like she was expendable. It was a well-known fact that we all very much disliked Allen; however, Simone disliked him with a fierce passion.

"What is he doing here?" Simone yelled.

Molly made a statement back in a tone that everyone knew would push Simone over the edge. "Well, he is my boyfriend. He has every right to come."

Without saying a word, Simone just walked away. She didn't yell or roll her eyes; she just silently walked over to the batting cages. I quickly headed over to her, along with Simone's boyfriend, Kyle.

"Hey you okay?" I asked, concerned.

"No!" she yelled. "You know I don't like him!"

"Hey, hey, hey, I know, but don't let him ruin your party. Let him stay. What's the worst that can happen," I started trying to sound convincing… but boy was I wrong.

After a few hours at Golf 'n' stuff, we headed off to The Loft for their screening version of *The Rocky Horror Picture Show*. I was a virgin to the show because I had never even seen the movie before.

For anyone who doesn't know exactly what this entails, allow me this moment to enlighten you. The movie is projected on screen just like any other theater, but actors join on stage in costume to reinact key moments of the movie, which at times involves audience participation. The worst part was when Allen found out where it was that we were going. He reacted in a way we never expected. He freaked out, and I mean F.R.E.A.K.E.D. O.U.T. He began to panic so bad that he started punching himself in the face.

"Well, that's not normal," I said in the middle of the group of people who were all open-mouth staring. After he calmed down, we rushed everyone inside, so we could catch our eight o'clock showing. All I could keep thinking was *Wow!* That show was a whole new kind of weird to me, but in the end, I actually liked it. It was the kind of strange excitement that my life needed at the moment. When the show had ended, so did the party, or at least for the boys. It was time for them to go home so that the girls could have a slumber party. Yes, this may sound childish, but what else do you call a group of girls spending the night all together at another friend's house?

Dean and I had talked the whole night, and for me, it was incredible. I had never clicked or felt such a connection with anyone like that before. It was like a drug, and I wanted more. Every time he moved, my gaze instantly went to him. I hung on every word. I felt truly happy for the first time in for as long as I could remember.

Earlier that night, I had pulled Simone to the side and had asked her what Dean's story was. To which she replied, "He is a great guy."

It was all she said and to me that meant he was available, so I decided that I would make a move. When everyone who wasn't staying overnight started to leave, I caught up to Dean and stopped him before he got to his car to leave. "Hey, where are you going?" I asked, and he turned around instantly and smirked. God, he was sexy, and oh my god, did I really just ask him where he was going? He wasn't a girl; I already knew where he was going.

To save me the embarrassment, he answered my question anyways. "Hey, I was just going to go pick up my girlfriend for the slumber party. She just got off work, so she couldn't make it until now."

As if the gods wanted to see fit that I was never happy, his words hit me like a sword, and it was weird because I felt the stab straight through my heart. He had a girlfriend, and why this information shocked me I'll never know because one, I had just met him, and two, it made total sense that he had a girlfriend; no one as sweet, kind, sexy, and perfect like him would ever be single. What did shock me the most was why Simone left out this important detail when I asked her earlier about him. Had he mentioned her before and I just didn't listen? How could I hit on a guy who had a girlfriend?

"Oh… well, have a good night. I hope we bump into each other again," I blurted out, trying not to sound as upset as I was. I couldn't get away fast enough, and I hoped that my embarrassment didn't show on my face.

Fifteen minutes later, Dean dropped off his girlfriend, Nicole. That whole night was very awkward; I felt awful for hitting on him, but I couldn't get him off my mind. Fortunately for me, this wouldn't be the last time that I'd see my forbidden Romeo, for we did indeed see each other again.

CHAPTER 2

The Reunion

We're given second chances every day of our life. We don't
usually take them, but they're there for the taking.
—Andrew M. Greeley

A whole month had gone by since Simone's birthday party, and the weather had change drastically; gone was the soothing rain, replaced by constant dry, sweltering heat. Today seemed to be another miserable hot day. It was an ordinary day for me, which was me locked in my room with my headphones in my ears and my music blaring. My chosen band for the day was Paramore, and I must have been lying on my bed for quite some time because by the time I came back to the world of the living, I felt like my whole body had sunk into my mattress. My phone started to buzz and move across my bed, and I quickly snatched it up before it hit the floor.

"Hello?" I answered in a way-too-perky tone because I was happy to have someone call me. I must have been more bored than I thought, I realized, as Simone greeted me on the other end who matched my perky tone.

"Hey, what you up to today?" she asked, and I knew she had another question to ask.

"The usual," I replied, the perkiness now drained from my tone.

"So you are locked in your room with your iPod on?" she asked, even though she knew me well enough to already know that she was right.

"Ha-ha, yes, and it's sad that I'm so predictable," I answered back, shaking my head.

"Well, that's because you don't get out enough, so how about Kyle and I can come to get you, and you can come over and go swimming at his house?" she asked all at once without even taking a single breath.

I sat up so fast that my sheets had no chance and ripped away from my back. "I'm so in," I perked up, desperately wanting to get out of my house.

Not too soon after hanging up with Simone, there was a honk from a car horn coming from the outside of my average suburban apartment. I ran to the front door, almost making my escape, when I heard my mother came up behind me.

"Where do you think you're going?" my mom asked in an alarming tone.

"Mom, I already told you I'm going swimming with Simone." I sighed, wishing my mother would just let me leave.

"Well, fine if you are going to do something today, then you can't do anything else for three days, and I want you to call in and check in every hour on the hour!" cautioned my mother.

"Are you serious? That's ridiculous. Why does it have to be three days? And how can I swim if I have to dry off to go into the house to call every hour?" I asked, gaping at my mother because her demands were getting worse and worse the older I got.

"I don't care, Hailey. Those are the rules, and you know that," she commanded.

The greatest part was I didn't get the memo for these new set of rules, but I knew better; to start a fight now would be suicide. Talking back would only see to it that I never saw daylight again. So

I would yet again deal with her new rules. I had to make the most of it, and hopefully, it will help me to get past the next three days.

"Yes, Mother," I muttered, sounding almost like a child, as I swiveled on my heel and ran toward the door with swimsuit in hand. I swung the door open and slammed it behind me. The moment I climbed into Kyle's white '95 Jeep Cherokee was when a smile finally crept across my face.

As we drove up to the house, I was amazed to see how well taken care of Kyle's house was, and this was just on the outside. It had white and purple flowers along the side of a concrete and brick pathway, which led to a small patio that was connected to the house. It had lush green grass that smelled just like a freshly cut soccer field. It was the only house on the entire block that had green grass and also the only house to have a garage. I was too distracted by observing my surroundings to realize that I was wearing flip flops on wet concrete, and just like that, *bam!* Flat on my ass is where I went.

"Are you okay?" I heard a voice ask, a voice I didn't recognize, but this voice seemed to pull at me, making me heart flutter. Wait. Yes, I did know this voice; with my eyes now closed tightly shut, I thought back. To the greatest and worst day of my life, the day I felt alive again and hollower than ever all at the same time. Back to a voice I spent a whole month trying to forget. Back to Simone's party. Back to Dean.

"Are you okay?" he asked again as I opened my eyes; his voice had a weird effect on me. His voice seemed to calm me and make my pulse race; it made me feel at peace. He made me feel whole.

"Well, besides a sore butt and being completely embarrassed, I'm great," I replied, trying to sound like I always did in order to not inform him as to what he did to me.

"Well, come on in. The pool is in the back," he remarked and pointed at the same time.

Simone led me to the back, and I couldn't help but to ask her what was on my mind. "What is Dean doing here?" I hoped I hadn't sounded rude.

"Didn't I tell you?" Simone asked quizzically. "Dean and I have been friends for years. He is also Kyle's brother. That's how Kyle and I met." *Well, that's just great*, I thought. My friend was dating Kyle, the brother of the guy who no matter how hard I tried I could never seem to forget. I was happy at the thought that this meant I would get to see him more often, yet at the same time, I didn't think my heart could handle it.

"Do you have somewhere I can change?" I asked Dean, holding up my bathing suit.

"Yeah, sure, follow me," he replied as he turned down a small hallway before suddenly stopping in front of a closed door. When he opened the door, it revealed a small bathroom that had everything you would need and just enough room for me to change in. I couldn't help but wonder how the hell someone as tall and muscular as Dean was ever able to move around in here.

After changing, I walked back out into the hallway to find it empty. *Now where do I go?* I asked as I wandered back down the hallway. Luckily, someone had left the patio door to the house open, so it wasn't long before I heard the sound of chatter and splashing. I headed toward the pool yard, and I kept thinking back to the turn of events that just unfolded. One, I fell on my ass in front of the cutest guy I've ever seen, and two, he was going to be around a lot more often, and that meant I'd be seeing more of him. In other words, I was totally screwed.

The gate surrounding the pool area sort of reminded me of prison bars; they had the same plain vertical design. As I opened the gate and let it shut behind me, it made a loud bang and clicking sound, alerting me that the gate was now locked firmly in place, which startled me. I looked toward the pool and saw that Simone and Kyle were the only ones there. I quickly took off the towel covering me, exposing my bathing suit and jumped into the pool, embarrassed that Dean might see me in my suit. I was showing more skin than I was used to because normally I'd wear a T-shirt and shorts over I;, however in my rush to get out of the house, I had forgotten both. I never have been confident in my looks, never saw myself as sexy nor beautiful, so I covered myself in order to prevent anyone from ever seeing. I would prefer to never have to see the look of disgust on someone's face if they saw what I did because let's face it, they can't fully judge what they can't see.

Minutes were ticking by, and Dean had still not come out to the pool area, and as for my other company, they weren't much of entertainment or conversation because they were in the corner of the pool yard, being all lovey. Deciding I didn't want to intrude, I started to do laps in the pool and had a good pace going; that was until we all heard a car door slam shut. It came from outside the front of the house, and a few seconds later, a tiny, thin guy walked through the pool yard gate. Standing there, he looked like a full-blown hippie; he had holes in his pants and was wearing a shirt that was a size too big. He had black medium-length hair, and an "I don't give a care" air in him. He had a goatee and looked like he hadn't showered in a few days. Introductions were given, and I soon found out this mystery guy's name was Joel and that he was one of Dean's best friends.

Soon after Joel's arrival, Dean had finally joined us. Everyone was swimming and having a good time. We went from playing Marco Polo to everyone doing their own thing, and I decided to go back to my laps, wanting to use this opportunity to get in some exercise to help better prepare me for when the soccer season started. After a few laps, someone grabbed me around my waist. At first, my only instinct was to panic because I was still underwater and had no idea who had me. I came shooting out of the water gasping for air and scrambled to the edge of the pool. I let out a gigantic cough, choking on the bitter taste of chlorine.

"Hey, are you okay? I'm sorry I was just playing around," my captor said, trying to apologize. After some struggle to get the blurriness from my eyes, I saw who was behind the silent attack in the pool.

"What, Joel?" I yelled because I didn't clearly hear his apology the first time.

"I said sorry," he stated clearly, a little upset. I felt sorry for being so angry at him because I now realized he was only trying to play around. I wanted Dean to like me, which meant his friends needed to like me too. So in order to lighten the mood, I decided to play back.

"Well, you're just lucky I wasn't on my A-game, or then you would really be in trouble," I stated.

"That sounds like a challenge," he retorted with a smooth smile on his face, and that was when the water battle began. I was having a lot of fun, and Joel was openly flirting with me, but I didn't flirt back because my mind kept drifting to one person... Dean. Whenever Joel started flirting with me, I would find some excuse to get away. Lucky my mother provided me with the perfect excuses; I kept leaving to check in with my mother. Every time I came back to the pool yard, Dean's name instantly came back to the forefront of my mind, and it kept ringing in my head almost like a chant. As I thought of his name yet again, my eyes swept over the pool scene and landed on his gaze, his staring gaze. My blood ran hot under his stare; why was he staring at me? Was it because Joel was flirting with me? I had to do a double take on Dean because for some stupid reason, I thought I saw jealousy in his eyes. I couldn't have read his emotions very well, but that look he was giving me sure looked like one of jealousy. If he were jealous, he shouldn't be; he had a girlfriend, didn't he? So why did he even care?

As soon as I broke eye contact with him, Dean jumped out of the pool and went into the house. Was he mad? Why did I care so much if he was? I needed to stop feeling for a guy who could never feel the same way. I was only torturing myself, setting myself up for heartache and pain. I had already invested too much of my feelings and thoughts on a man who belonged to someone else. The only thing I could think to do was to go back to hanging out with Joel, Simone, and Kyle hopefully to distract myself, even if it was only temporarily. A few minutes passed by when Dean's voice echoed in the pool yard.

"Watch out below!" his voice rang. It sounded close but far away all at once. From the corner of my eye, I saw some movement, and that's when I spotted him. Wow, he was just as gorgeous as he was that night. I quickly shook that thought from my head. Why was I focusing on how he looked when he was standing on the roof of his house? What was he doing up there? As if he knew what I thought, he started to back up and got a running start. He jumped off aiming straight for the middle of the pool, forming a perfect cannonball. He disappeared, and left in his place was a mushroom cloud of water.

He didn't come up for a few seconds, and I had hoped he hadn't hurt himself. All of a sudden, I heard a single word, "Hey," come from behind me. I turned around so quickly that the water swished into little waves around me. I turned around to find Dean now smiling in front of me. I felt like a complete idiot because no words would come out of my mouth.

"He isn't right for you," Dean stated, quickly glancing over to Joel. Without saying anything either, Joel just swam away, leaving Dean and me to take in each other. He just kept staring at me, and I couldn't read anything in his stare. I know that my stare was one of confusion. Every time I think I have this crazy fascination with Dean under control, he would do or say something that would send me spiraling down the rabbit hole. "I know I shouldn't, but I don't like the way he looks at you either," he whispered still holding my gaze.

When Dean finally glanced away, we separated and went on to do our own thing for the rest of the time that was spent in the pool. What do you say after something like that? I spent the rest of my time in the pool lost deep in thought. I felt like such a loser, wanting someone who could never want me and letting him affect me so much that I felt like I was beginning to lose myself. After a while, we all decided to head back inside, and after drying off, we headed to the kitchen. We were all sitting around eating whatever junk food we could get our hands on, and I had zoned out yet again, which was starting to become a new hobby of mine ever since I met Dean.

"Hey, Hailey, I asked you a question," Simone spoke again, but a little higher up than before.

I snapped out of my thoughts. "Sorry, what did you ask?" I asked, feeling bad for not paying attention yet again.

"I asked how come you never text anyone on your phone? Didn't you just get one? Isn't that why you got one so you could text people?" Simone asked.

I couldn't help but wonder how we went from talking about our upcoming classes to this. Weren't we just talking about the worst teachers we ever had? I really had to stop zoning out, like I was doing right now yet again. *Crap, what is wrong with me?* Plus Simone knew I didn't have that many friends, just the ones in our close circle, and not all of them had cell phones. So why was she asking me this? If there was one thing I knew about Simone was that whenever she did or said something weird, it was generally because she had something up her sleeve.

"Um, I don't know honestly. I guess it's because I don't have that many people to text, or maybe no one wants to text me that much. Other than you and the few girls on the team, I don't have many friends," I stated when I finally realized they were waiting for me to reply.

"Well, you can text me if you want."

I swallowed hard, hoping that I hadn't imagine the words I had just heard, and I had hoped even more that I hadn't imagine who I had heard the words come from. I looked over in Dean's direction, hoping that he was the one who had said the comment.

"So what's your number?" he asked as he pulled out his phone. As I gave him my number, I couldn't contain all the hope I had that he would actually text me.

As it started to get late, Simone and I had begun to get ready because it was time for us to go home. As we piled back into Kyle's car, I kicked myself mentally for not remembering to grab Dean's number before I left, and all of a sudden, I felt as though I probably would never hear from him.

Ding, ding, ding, ding! My phone went off, and I flipped it open and saw a blinking light that stated I had a new message.

"Hey, what's up. It's Dean," the message read.

I must have reread that line six times because I just couldn't believe that he would text me. I had just pulled away from the house with Simone and Kyle, and he had texted me first! I cannot believe he had text me so soon.

"Hey, nothing much," was what I wrote back, for it was the only thing I could think of to say because my mind was racing.

No more than a minute later, I received this message: "You know, if we're going to be friends and message each other a lot, then you're going to need to be that girl you were the night of Simone's party and talk to me."

Had I been acting that different since the party that he had noticed it? And why did it seem like it bugged him that I was acting differently? I was of course acting different at Simone's party; I was under the belief that he was single, so I did something I normally never do; I let me guard down in order to let someone else in. Well, none of that mattered because I did need to start acting like myself because all I knew was I wanted him in my life even if it was just as a friend.

Two months went by in a blink of an eye; all Dean and I did was text and talk. We went to each other with all our problems and thoughts, and I did the one thing I swore I wouldn't do: I fell in love with him. Even though he wasn't mine to fall in love with. I just couldn't help it; he knocked down every defense I had. Worse, everything about him called to me—his personality, his sense of humor, but most of all, his kindness. We would talk, a lot. I mean we talked so much we stayed up until five in the morning and did not even realize it. We would pass out, and we always seemed to wake up at the same time; most of the time, we were up at seven in the morning, and we would do it the next day all over again. We talked about anything and everything. He had become my best friend; I knew I could trust him with anything, even my heart. He wouldn't laugh; he never thought I was weird even though I knew I was.

Our conversations were always platonic. He was very loyal to his girlfriend, and even though we wrote all the time, we never did or said anything inappropriate. I respected his feelings and his girlfriend. I never wanted to be the reason why two people broke up; so even though I let him in, started to love him, I became what he needed as a friend, and that's all. He never told any of my secrets to anyone, and his friendship made me so happy, but my happiness wouldn't last for long

CHAPTER 3

My Christmas Miracle

Never lose hope, my dear heart. Miracles dwell in the invisible.
—Rumi

"What do you mean you are shutting my phone off!" I screamed at my mother.

You could feel the tension in the air; it felt so thick you could probably cut it with a knife, and I could imagine that our neighbors could hear the screaming match that was taking place.

"I have to Hailey!" she screamed back, and that was final. There was no way I was winning this argument. An anger I never felt before rose in me, and I had to take some deep calming breaths before I did or said something I regretted.

"Well, can I at least text my friends to tell them what's going on?" I begged. There was only one person I wanted to text, and that was Dean; he was the only person I felt like I couldn't go without texting.

"No, give me the phone now!" she yelled, and I panicked as I handed her the phone. A sad truth rang through my head: I could no longer talk to Dean anymore. I didn't know what I was going to do anymore. Dean was my salvation, the person I went to with my thoughts and concerns. He was my escape from my fears, the escape from the things my mother would say to bring me down, and now I could no longer text him any time I wanted to.

The next month was hard without Dean. Not having a phone limited the contact we had with each other. We tried to talk on Myspace as much as we could, but it never seemed like enough for me. The only thing that helped pass the long days were the songs we sent back and forth to each other. It was a way we could share our feelings without having to talk.

I rolled over in bed and stared back at my flashing alarm clock. *Great, the electricity went out again last night. That is what happens when you live in a hellhole like this,* my inner voice sneered. I shot up in bed and scrambled for my watch. *Whew! It's only nine o'clock. I didn't miss Myspace time with Dean.* Dean and I made an agreement to meet online at ten o'clock in the morning every day so we can talk as long as we could during winter break. The moment I logged on, my inbox dinged at me.

"Hailey, I got up early to send this to you because I have to help my parents today so I can't talk to you today. Here's my song to you today. I hope you understand what I am trying to say."

I was disappointed that we weren't able to talk today, but my heart always sped up whenever I listen to a song he has chosen. Music had always spoken to me on many levels because it could take that one perfect song to turn my whole day around. It was also a way for me to say how I felt without me actually saying it. If anyone cared enough to learn, someone could always tell how I was feeling by the song or type of music I was listening to. A part of me like to believe that Dean cared, and that's why he suggested we share songs with each other.

"'Damn Regret' by the Red Jumpsuit Apparatus. Never heard of them," I murmured as I read the song that Dean had sent me. I instantly looked up the song and focused hard to hear the words. My heart froze on the first few lyrics: "I'll kiss you on your neck, people will stare, but we won't care."

I pushed any thoughts aside because I didn't want to read too much into it until I heard more of the song. Then my heart nearly exploded when I heard the next words: "You're the only one I turn to, when I feel like no one's there." What did that mean? Does he like me as a friend? Or did he maybe like me more than that? Could it possibly be that he feels the same way as I do about us no longer being able to text every day?

I did the only thing I could. I sent him back a song to say what I couldn't. Before logging off, I wrote, "Great song! I know how you're feeling! The song spoke to me as well. Here's mine." I sent him a song by the same band he sent me. I sent him "Your Guardian Angel." I hope that when he heard this song, he knew no matter what, I was there for him, and I would show him that I was the one and only for him. I knew that he still had a girlfriend, and no matter how rocky their relationship was, I could and would never make an advance. Yet no matter how hard I tried, I couldn't help my feelings, so I would continue to be whatever Dean needed me to be.

After that, we didn't talk nearly as much as we used to, and I was lucky to receive a single message from him a day. It made me miss so many things; I missed our late night and early morning chats. I missed how he would ask me how my day was. I missed the random messages he sent. I missed the excitement I got when I would see that I have a message from him. I missed everything about him; then I felt a sharp pain in my heart, and it felt like my heart shattered into a million pieces. I realized why I missed him so much. I really and truly had fallen in love with Dean.

It felt as though I always had been and was going to be forever in love with him that for me there would never be another. I was in love with a man who was with someone else, and I was in love with a man who I couldn't even share my true feelings with. I knew this sounded dramatic and extreme considering I was only sixteen, but I just knew that he was it, the other half of me and that there would never be anyone else like him.

Weeks passed, and I had finally saved up enough to buy a pay-as-you-go phone, plus a minute card, and the first thing I did was text Dean. "Hey, it's Hailey. How have you been?"

The few seconds that passed waiting for his reply felt like an eternity. Instead of a text message, I received a phone call from him. "Hey, I'm great now. Whose phone are you using?"

"It's mine," I replied. "It's a pay-as-you-go phone."

"No way! So we get to talk like we used to in the old days?" he responded happily.

"The old days?" I replied, and I couldn't help but laugh. "You make it sound like it's been forever. And sadly, no, because now I have limited minutes, but if it means I get to talk to you, I'll just buy more," I replied quickly, not wanting to make him sad because I would do whatever it took to continue to talk to him. "So how are you and Nicole?" I asked, trying to change the subject while sounding nonchalant.

"Not so good. I think she's cheating on me," he said sounding upset, and I couldn't understand how girls like Nicole get guys like Dean. Girls who would so easily throw away a great guy for some cheap thrill. This was Dean's third relationship, and the past two girls ended up cheating on him. I could never understand how girls like them could get so lucky to have an amazing guy like Dean just to throw it away by cheating. If I was his girlfriend, I would never betray him like that. I would thank fate every day for giving me even a second to be with him.

"What are you going to do?" I asked concerned.

"I don't know. Do you think I should leave her?" he asked.

I was speechless. What do I say to something like that? I could say the truth of what was in my heart and my mind, and the answer I wanted to say was yes, that I did think he should leave her. She didn't deserve him because she didn't respect, understand, or love him. That he deserved to be with someone who would love him with everything she had, who would be honest with him. I wanted him to be with me so bad, but I could never tell him that. Right now, he needed a friend. He needed me to be just a friend. So I lied. "Well, that's not for me to decide. You need to listen to your heart or wait until you have proof," I said, answering his question the best way I knew, even though, it tore me apart inside to not being able to tell him how I truly felt.

"Thanks, buddy," he said, and from his reply, I could tell I had made him happier. But ouch. Those two words nearly did killed me.

After reconnecting, we talked as much as we could, and I found out firsthand that pay-as-you-go phones were horrible. They ate through your minutes extremely fast. Ten cents a minute for phone calls and ten cents a text eventually added up, especially with how much Dean and I talked.

A week after our conversation on the phone, I received a text from Dean that changed everything. "Nicole and I are done for good. I need a friend. Can we hang out?"

"Yeah, of course," I replied as quickly as I possibly could.

Dean made the thirty-minute drive to come and pick me up. After only being in his car for only ten minutes, I was doing all I could to be a good friend as he told me what had happen.

"She came over to hang out, and I noticed that she was wearing this large scarf. That wasn't as odd as the fact that she was over for an hour and had still not taking it off. Eventually I grew tired of being suspicious, so I took her scarf off... That's when I noticed that her neck was completely covered in hickeys. I know I sure as hell was not the one to put them there," Dean stated as he took a deep breath to calm the angry tremor in his voice. "When I asked her what the hell was on her neck, she tried to tell me her dad pinch her neck so hard it left those marks. I can't believe she thought I was so stupid that I would actually fall for that," Dean said, shaking his head. "It turned into a fight, and the worst part is that this all happen in front of Kyle and Joel. Kyle even went as far as to pinch Joel's neck multiple times to prove that it wasn't possible." Dean sighed.

I stayed quiet, knowing he was far from done, that he had only just begun to purge his system of the hate and betrayal that was coursing through him.

"I can't believe she cheated on me. Did she think that I was so stupid that I wouldn't figure it out?" He was starting to yell now, and I could feel the anger rising as tension filled the car.

"Hey, no, you're not stupid. Trust me when I say she is the stupid one. Anyone would be lucky to have you." I practically shouted, matching his tone, hoping he could hear me through his haze, and by the time I had realized what I had said, it was too late to take it back. I realized at that moment I might have said too much.

"You mean that?" he asked, and he finally smiled for the first time since he came to pick me up. It was that smile that always made me melt, and I know it always would.

"Hell yeah, I know I would be!" I shouted out before I could stop myself. *Oh my god, oh my god. Shut up, shut up. Stick your foot in your mouth before you say anymore then you should!* I said, screaming at myself in my head.

It was quiet for a while, and I was beginning to worry that I had finally said too much, and because of me, our friendship would be over. Then like a raging dragon that broke through the silence, I heard, "I like you."

I looked at him quickly with huge wide eyes, wondering if I had heard him correctly. *Say something quick*, I thought. "I like you too. I have for a long time, and you are my best friend," I said, looking down at my hands. Good, everything was fine. I didn't ruin everything. I knew that when he said that he liked me, he meant only as a friend as he has always liked me. That when he said he liked me, he was only trying to let me down easily. So instead of troubling him with my feelings, I hid them in my walled-up heart and lied.

In a nervous tone, Dean finally spoke, "No, I like you more than that!"

Was this a dream? This had to be.. No way someone like Dean, who was kind, loving, and to me, perfect in every way, would like someone like me. I wasn't pretty by any means. I was average and broken. I had demons and a darkness in me that I feared would prevent me from ever being able to love and be loved in return. I knew what love was and what it felt like, but it takes more than that to truly love someone. You must give yourself entirely to someone, letting them in to the very dark corners of your heart and mind. If Dean saw the true me, how broken I was, I feared he wouldn't be able to love me. Even so, I couldn't stop myself from pinching myself trying to wake up from what felt like a dream.

"Are you going to say something?" he asked, and I raised my head instantly to look into his eyes and saw his look of panic. I knew then what I really had to do. I had to lay everything I was and everything I felt out in front of him. To truly let him in 100 percent and hope that what he saw didn't scare him away. So I took a deep breath and said how I really felt.

"I like you a lot more than just as a friend too, and I meant it when I said that I had liked you for a while," I said and covered my face quickly, hoping to hide my burning face, feeling like such a loser because I made myself sound so desperate. My face just continued to get redder at the thought that I had just been open with my feelings to Dean and that I was about to share more. "I have had a crush on you since the day we met, but I shove them away because you had a girlfriend, and I rather have you in my life as a friend than not at all." I took a depth breath and took the final leap. "Two weeks ago, you asked me why I haven't dated anyone, and I told you this lame excuse that there was no one interested in dating me. Well, that was bullshit. I didn't date anyone because no one was ever good enough. They weren't you."

"Wow, it's a relief to hear you say that," he said. "This may sound bad, but I have liked you too for a while, and I felt so guilty for wanting you when I was with someone else. I liked Nicole, but I couldn't stop thinking about you. I stayed with her only because I was afraid to tell you how I felt because you may not have felt the same way. She was a distraction, and I know that makes me a coward. I never acted on my feelings for you because of my respect for Nicole, but I also shouldn't have stayed with someone I couldn't give myself fully to. I had some feelings for her. That's probably why her betrayal still hurt. However, I never felt for her what I feel for you. Now that I know how you, feel my heart feels lighter, but… I'm not going to ask you out just yet," he said thoughtfully as he looked me in the eye.

I was speechless. I didn't know what to think or say. If he liked me and I liked him, then why couldn't we date?

"Don't get too sad. I meant it when I said I liked you. I do, a lot. I like you enough to respect you too much to jump into a relationship with you on the same day Nicole and I broke up. I don't want you to be the rebound girl because rebound relationships never work, and to be truthful, I want us to work, more than I've wanted anything else in my life."

Once he was done talking, just like that, I was on cloud nine. Even though a part of me was disappointed that we weren't going out now. I was so happy that he thought I meant more than a onetime fling, that I meant more to him than someone he could have used to forget about Nicole. Because sadly I would have let him. If it meant that I got to have some part of him, I would take anything. Even if it was for a short period of time, then I would always have something to carry around with me, locked away inside my soul that I knew would be only mine and that no one could take it away. However what he said sounded even more amazing, and I realized that he was a better person than I ever imagine because most guys would have taken the opportunity to hook up with the next girl that came along. Maybe that's why Dean had caught my eye, why I fell in love with him so easily. Why before him there had never been anyone else. He was different than most guys; he was one of a kind.

More days came to pass as Dean and I started to hang out a lot more often. He would make the long drive down to my house every day just to see me, even if it was only for a few minutes. It felt so good just to spend time with Dean. I felt more at ease around him because I now knew where we stood. I was still a nervous wreck, waiting for him to ask me out, and I knew that I wouldn't feel better until we became official. Until I could truly call him mine.

One night, when we couldn't hang out because my mother wouldn't allow me to, we were on the phone playing one of our favorite games. We called it infinity questions, a lot like twenty-one questions but instead of trying to question what thing someone was thinking, it was a way we could figure out what the other was truly thinking. It also gave us a way to ask the questions that were on our mind but we sometimes were too afraid to ask. Dean called it infinity questions, but it was more like ask questions until you can't anymore. The rules of the game were simple: one person would ask the other a question, and that person had to answer it honestly no matter what. There was no room for embarrassment, and Dean and I trusted each other enough to believe that we would answer each other's question honestly. Dean liked to ask easy questions first before asking the harder ones. I however asked the most difficult question first because that question would always be the one that had been on my mind for days, and when I asked it, it was only because I had finally worked up the nerve to do it.

"I was wondering when you were going to ask me out?" I asked, hoping that my question wouldn't end up making him mad.

"And I was wondering when you were going to ask me that. I know you, Hailey, and unfortunately you don't have very much patience," he said, obviously trying to not answer my question, and he stayed silent on the other end of the phone for a while.

"Why do you want to date me so much anyways?" he asked, not sounding mad but instead he seemed sad, as if he was afraid to know my answer. As if he doubted that someone could want him as much as I did and in the way that I did.

I always knew my answer, and I didn't stop to think about it at all before I replied. Didn't think of the consequence or that maybe by sharing this I would be sharing too much. I jumped and hoped he would catch me. "Because I love you." And before I could explain my response, I was met with the dial tone. I tried to call and text him, hoping the call had dropped or that his phone had died, but I didn't receive a text or call from him for the rest of the night, and I knew I might have just scared him away... possibly for good.

The day was December 25, Christmas Day, and boy was I in desperate need of a Christmas miracle. Last night, I confessed my true feelings by telling the boy I loved that I was head over heels for him. It had been six months since our confessions in Dean's car, and I was afraid that I had said too much too soon. I hadn't heard from him all day, and as I looked at the clock and saw it read ten o'clock, I feared that I'd never hear from him again. Twenty-four hours was a long time, and I thought that Dean might be avoiding me because if his phone died or broke, he would have found a way to contact me by now.

I nearly fell off my bed when Dean's ringtone, "Iris" by the Goo Goo Dolls, went off. I lunged across the room and answered it with a panting

"Hello!"

"Hi, Hailey," Dean's voice came in on the other end, and my heart started pounding loudly.

"Oh, I'm sorry, do I know you? You sound an awful lot like my best friend Dean, which is a funny story because I confessed my love to him last night. But you couldn't possibly be him because he left me in the dark for almost twenty-four hours," I shouted trying not to be mad, but I couldn't help feeling hurt. "I'm sorry, that was mean, but seriously, what happened to you?"

"I'm sorry my phone died last night… " he whispered back, starting to sound like he was going to make excuses. "And I guess I also got a little scared away last night, and I'm sorry that wasn't fair. I know how much courage it took to tell me how you feel. I had to think about me, you, and us last night. You are such an amazing person, and I wanted to make sure I was the right person for you. I realized how much I don't want to lose you, so will you please go out with me?" he stated so fast, probably in the hopes that it wouldn't give me any opportunity at all to interrupt him.

My heart raced again, but this time in a good way. I felt my heart get lighter, and somewhere inside, it felt like my beaten and torn heart mended a little. I knew that no matter how happy I was, I needed to have Dean sweat it out a little because of how he made me sweat it out last night after my confession to him. So I put on my most innocent voice to answer his question.

"Where did you want to go to? The store?"

"Come on, Hailey, don't be a smart-ass." He laughed. "You know exactly what I'm asking," he said, waiting nervously for my answer.

"Hell yes!" I screamed. "That's my answer, hell yes, you didn't even have to ask. You could have just assumed we were dating."

"Okay! I'm on my way. I have to see you!" he exclaimed, and then with a click, I knew he had disconnected the call.

I was so happy I started to geek out and dance in my room even though there was no music playing. The dance was short lived as a few seconds later, my mother stormed into the room.

"Hailey, what is going on? Why are you in here screaming?" Helga shouted.

"Sorry, Mom," I apologized sincerely. "I was screaming because Dean just asked me out, and I am utterly euphoric."

"And you said yes?" my mother asked like I had just made a stupid mistake.

"Why wouldn't I say yes? Mom, you know how much I like him," I said puzzled.

"Well, I do not approve of this. You can't see him because I didn't choose him for you, Hailey!"

"But, Mother, I love him, and you can't choose who I can and cannot love. He is on his way over now, Mom. Please don't ruin this for me. I tried dating someone you chose, and it didn't work," I pleaded with my mother.

"He can't come over, and if you leave this house, I will ground you until you're eighteen," my mom cautioned, grinning, looking as though she just won the argument.

"You know what, Mother," I exploded, "I'm sorry, but enough is enough. I will see him because I love him, and this might sound silly to you, but he is the one. My heart knows there will never be another. You have no control over me anymore, and if you don't learn to approve of this, I will walk out of your life forever."

My mom stood there opened mouth at the end of my small speech. "You don't know what real love is, Hailey. I can look at you and know that this love is only temporary."

Before I could retort, the doorbell rang, and I grabbed my purse in the same instant as I headed past my mother toward the front door. My hand grasped the handle so tight my knuckles turned white. With my hand still wrapped around the door handle, I turned toward my mother and enjoyed the look on her face, realizing that I was serious and I was actually leaving. Yet before I left the house, I told her, "Maybe it's you, Mother, who doesn't know what love is."

I stayed out with Dean almost the entire night before I decided I was ready to go home. We took as much time as we could and walked at a slow pace up to my front door.

"Are you sure you're going to be okay?" Dean asked with concern on his face.

"Honestly, this might sound weird, but now that I have something worth fighting for, I will not let her take it from me. You have given me a reason to live, a reason to believe," I confessed.

"Did I not do that before?" Dean asked.

"In a way, yes, but now it's so much more because now you're mine." I blushed.

Then he leaned forward, stopping just inches from my lips. We stood there breathing each other in, and before the longing became unbearable, our lips touched. This was my first real kiss. I mean, I had kissed a boy before, but the thing was that when I kissed someone before, it felt like two lips touching, that's all; it lasted no more than a second, but that wasn't a real kiss. This kiss made the world stop and the earth move. It made my skin heat up and my heart on the verge of exploding. I leaned more into him as his mouth still continued to take possession of mine. I wrapped my arms around him, trying for some reason to get even closer, and that's when the kiss finally came to an end.

"I love you," Dean whispered, and he kissed me again.

CHAPTER 4

Moving In

*True love is an act of the will—a conscious decision to do
what is best for the other person instead of ourselves.*
—Billy Graham

Ding dong! rang the door, waking me from my sleep. The next thing I
heard was a muffled conversation that came from downstairs, waking
me fully from my sleep.

"Oh, hey, Dean. Let me go get Hailey," announced Helga.

"Thank you, Helga" Dean replied politely to my mother.

Dean and I had been together for nearly a month, and it had
been the best month of my life. I could tell my mom wasn't a hundred percent happy with my relationship with Dean, but she had
come to accept the fact that I wasn't going to give him up. Not without one hell of a fight, and if there was one thing my mom hated, it
was a fight. She tried to limit the time I had with Dean as much as
she can, but we always found a way around that. My friends would
say that I was at their house, but I was most likely at Dean's, but I
always made some time for my friends too. I know that it was bad to
lie to her, and a part of me felt bad for doing it, but this was the first
time in my life that I ever truly wanted anything, and I was not going
to let her take it from me. Not like she has done before, I have always
followed her rules, but not anymore.

I heard my mom coming up the stairs as I peered at the clock; it was seven. Dean was on time again, like he was every morning he came to pick me up. My mom may have actually disliked Dean and me spending so much time together, but when Dean offered to take me to school every day, my mom was too lazy to refuse. This gave us more time to hang out with each other. My mom was under the impression that I had a zero period class. A zero period took place in the hour before school normally started and was often used for extracurricular classes or college-based classes. I had originally signed up for yearbook for my zero period but quickly learned that it wasn't for me. Turned out yearbook was mostly about popularity, so I dropped the class. I didn't want to disappoint my mom or make her angry at me, so I never told her. Dean would come and pick me up in the morning at seven, and we would hang out before my first period start. A part of me felt sorry for lying to my mother, but when my mom would put me down, it made me feel better about lying. I lied because I now had something in my life that made me feel good about myself, and I now had someone that believed in me. Dean made me feel like I was important and worthy of someone's love.

Instead of me going to school, we went over to Dean's house because it was down the street from my school. There we would watch a movie or have breakfast together. We would have hung out at school, but Dean was no longer in high school. He had decided to graduate a year early and officially graduated during my freshman year. The best thing about our plan was that after school, my mom let us hang out because she thought we weren't spending any other time together. He was such a sweet boyfriend, picking me up every day from school, even then he was on time so I was never left waiting. Unfortunately, in my life, good things tend to not last very long.

"Hailey, I have set up a few new rules for you and that boyfriend of yours!" my mother exclaimed, blindsiding me one morning.

"He has a name, Mother!" I voiced, getting mad at my mom again because I hated how she wouldn't address Dean by his name to me. She would almost always address him as "him" or "your boyfriend."

She ignored my comment and went on ranting her new rules. "You have to spend two days home before you can spend one day with Dean. Also, I don't think I like you two being alone at his house. I don't like the fact that his mother runs her house like a whorehouse."

I looked at my mom in disbelief. I never understood how she could say things like that. Dean's mother, Constantine, was a great and kind person; she loved her kids and supported them. She fed half the neighborhood's kids and always had a place for her kid's friends to sleep if they couldn't go home or weren't allowed to. She ran things differently than most parents, but the way she figured it was that her kids would find a way to do what they want, no matter what. If she were understanding, they would be truthful with her, and she was right, she had six fantastic kids. Her way of thinking made sense even if it is orthodox, but that in no way meant she was running her house like a whorehouse.

I also understood that my mother wanted me home; most parents wanted to see their kids. However that wasn't the case with my mother; she just wanted control. If she truly wanted me home because she wanted to see more of me, then she could just communicate with me or every once in a while invite Dean to come over, even if it was just for dinner, but that was never going to happen. I started to try and refute my mom, but before I could, she held up her index finger.

"If you fight me on these new rules, I will take away the privilege of you seeing him, period, and I can because I am your guardian until your eighteen." She smiled smugly.

She was right, so I ran past my mom and down the stairs as fast as I could because I knew I couldn't change or fight anything she said no matter how outrageous and unfair it was. Dean was already waiting in his Jeep for me, and I couldn't wait till I got into his car so I could kiss those perfect sweet lips and drown in his kiss, forgetting everything. I could ignore the fact I lived with a hurtful person and remind myself that I now had someone I could call all my own. Someone who loved me as much as I loved them.

My mom was quick on my heels, and I jumped in Dean's car, hoping he would speed away, but I was amazed when Dean rolled down his car window to speak to my mother.

"Hey, Mrs. Wyatt?" Dean's voice rang over the car engine and broke through my confusion.

"Yes?" my mother replied, sounding as curious as I was.

"I was wondering if after Hailey got out of school and of course after her game today if I could take her, you, Melvin, and Ross to a treat tonight?"

I couldn't help but wonder why Dean wanted to treat my parents and my brother to a treat on one of our few days to spend together.

"How does dinner out sound?"

And the conversation fell silent after the question was asked.

Then Dean added, "I'm buying, of course."

"Oh, that would be great. It sounds like we would all have a lot of fun," my mother replied with happiness. I found it funny how my mom became excited when Dean had offered to pay for dinner.

"I'll see you later, Mrs. Wyatt." Dean honked as we pulled away from the house; if any good comes from this, maybe my mom would reconsider this new rule she established.

When we were a good safe distance down the road, I turned toward him and let lose my concern. "What the hell was that? You invited my mom, my dad, and my brother to come hang out with us. Thanks to my mom's new rule, we only have one day together, then two without each other… " I paused. "Sorry, I didn't mean to get frustrated with you, and I know you didn't know that. It's just… you know how crazy my mother makes me." I felt sorry for getting mad, I did; but I didn't want to spend my alone time with Dean, after my game, with my whole family. I only wanted to be with Dean tonight, but my private pity party didn't last long.

"Baby, calm down. I did it for a reason. I would only ask your family somewhere with us only if I had to. Which I do, because I, sweetheart, have a plan," he said, trying to reassure me, and then he smiled the crooked side smile that always reached his eyes. It was that same smile that made me fall in love with him on day one. That damn smile still drove me crazy and made my heart flutter.

"What plan? Why do you need to have a plan?" I asked excitedly, now in a better mood.

"You'll see, this plan has a purpose, and it will work because all I know is I can't stand to be away from you."

No matter how many times I asked, this is the only answer I got out of him.

"Oh, by the way, happy birthday, baby," he said and kissed me on the cheek, and I knew it was his attempt to stop me from asking any more questions. This only worked because with the morning's events, I had totally forgotten what day it was. What was even worse was that even though my dad and I shared the same birthday, my mother either forgot my birthday altogether or didn't care enough to acknowledge it.

Before getting out of the car, Dean handed me an envelope with my name on it and leaned close to whisper in my ear. "Don't open it till you get to class." Again, I felt that pull in my heart as if my heart repaired itself a little more. As I left his car, I took one last look back at my future.

As I sat down at my desk in my first-period class, I looked around and saw my other classmates having conversations with each other, so as always I kept to myself. I looked down at Dean's letter, and I knew I wasn't alone anymore. I couldn't help but wish that our

time together this morning lasted longer. I slowly opened the envelope, wanting to be careful with it. In the envelope were two pieces of
paper. One, a drawing, and the other, a letter. I opened the letter first
because the letters Dean wrote me were always amazing. At the top
of the letter, it read, "My Want List." Reading this instantly brought
a smile to my face. This was something Dean and I would do often.
We would take a piece of paper and write down a list of things we
want in the future. I continued to read down Dean's list:

All
I
Want
Is
An
Eternity
Of
Happiness
With
You!
Nothing
Else
Matters
As long
As
I
Have
You!
Forever and always.

Tears started to form in my eyes, and I quickly brushed them
away. I opened the drawing next. On the outside of the drawing,
it read "Happy birthday" in colorful big letters. Then there was a

Celtic drawing of a heart with writing in the middle of it. What he had written on the heart calmed my racing mind and soothed any fears I might have had. Just three simple words made everything that was upside down in my world right again. "I love you." The last time Dean had said that he loved me was nearly a month ago when we kissed for the first time. I pulled out my cell phone because I wanted to text him as fast as I could. "I love you too," and I pressed send; then I shut my phone off, ready to take on whatever the day brought.

After school, I met Dean in the same spot that we always met at; it was in a parking lot that was located right across our school. It was a parking lot that belonged to a pizza joint.

"Hey, babe." Dean smirked as he greeted me.

"Hey to you too," I chuckled as I wrapped my arms around Dean.

"You excited about your game?" Dean asked, pulling away so he could look into my eyes.

"Yes,, even more so than usual, but that may be because it is the first time you're seeing me play." I grinned.

"Well, I wanted to give you something for good luck," Dean whispered, and as our eyes locked, Dean took a step closer. It felt as though electricity coursed between us, a feeling I was becoming more and more familiar with. Dean's arms drifted around my waist, pulling me tighter against his body so that mine was flushed against his. I kissed him harder, fueled by my hunger for him. It was him who was the first to pull away, and even though that kiss lasted merely a few seconds, it would echo in my soul forever.

After our scorching make-out session, I was hesitant to head back inside. It was only after Dean had promised that he would see me at my game that I finally headed back toward school to go get ready for my game.

I walked up to my locker and sat my old yellow gym bag down on the wooden bench in front of our locker. After playing soccer for six years, I still had the same bag; and even though it looked well used, I never had the heart to get a new one. I closed my eyes and took a deep breath as I began my pregame ritual. I pulled out my silver-and-black iPod and stuck an earbud in each ear. I turned the volume up to almost the maximum volume in order to get in the right state of mind and also to prevent anyone from distracting me. No one really understood why I needed to do this, but as goalie, I felt I needed to be totally focused. Nothing else mattered but the game; if I was distracted, I might miss a ball, and that wasn't fair to my team. They trusted me to do everything in my power to stop the other team from scoring. I scrolled through my iPod until I found the play-list I was looking for. My game soundtrack started to play; first song up was "Let the Bodies Hit the Floor" by Drowning Pool. I changed quickly into my soccer uniform as the lyrics coursed through me.

I placed my backpack and clothes into my locker, and after receiving a text from Dean that read "Good luck," I put my cell phone in the locker as well. My next step was to get all my gear on, so I made sure that my uniform was in proper order and carefully place on my shin guards. Having put on the knee-high soccer socks over my shin guards, I put on my soccer cleats and began tightening the laces on my shoes. This was always the hardest part because I needed to make sure they were tight enough that they wouldn't fall off, yet without them being too tight that they would hurt my feet. Next, I made sure to wrap each one of my fingers individual and properly with bandage tape before placing on my goalie gloves. By doing this, it ensured that I wouldn't jam my fingers or break them. By the time I had finished getting ready, I had listened to almost six songs on my playlist before finally taking my earbuds out. I looked around the locker room and saw the rest of the girls looking back, and that was our cue to head out to the field.

Before our team stepped onto the field, my team and I do our pregame tradition together, where we stand side by side and hop three times on our right foot. After making the sign of the cross on our chest, we take our positions on the field. Other than for superstitious reasons, we never understand why we truly did it. During our freshman year, we had hit a losing streak. One of the girls on the team had suggested our ritual as a way to do something fun in the hopes of lifting our spirits. We won our first game that year, so we did it from that day forward. This was the game of the year for me; not only was it our last and final game, but it was also my birthday and the first game Dean would be at. I stood in goal, and my heart started pumping.

Before Dean, this game was my life. I lived, breathed, ate, slept, and dreamt soccer. The game was off to a good start, and by the second half, we were only behind by two points. I could see the team's spirit and energy run low, and as team captain, I was doing all I could to motivate them.

"Come on, girls, you got this!" I shouted to encourage my team.

The other team was able to steal the ball from our front fielder, and the opposite team began to make their way toward our goal. Our team did all we could to defend the goal, but the opposite team still slipped through, and I tensed my body, bracing myself for their shot. My pulse raced, and my breathing spiked as adrenaline coursed threw me, turning my body into a live wire. That's when the player struck, kicking the ball high, aiming for the left side of the goal post. I leaped to the left just quick enough to tip the ball outside of the goal. My team went crazy, leaping in the air, and I knew that I had just given my team the boost they needed to stay in this game.

The game was ticking down to its final minutes, and we were now tied, four to four. I could hear Dean cheering for me and the rest of the team. A smile spread across my face as I stepped up to the goalie's kicking line and punted the ball to the halfway line of the field, right into the kicking range of my teammate who after some fancy footwork made a score on the opposite teams goal.

Before my team and I could celebrate, the referee called a penalty, stating that a member of our team had pushed down a member from the opposite team; lucky for us, our recently scored point still counted. The player who had been pushed down walked up to the penalty kick line and waited until the referee placed the ball on the line at her feet. It was moments like this that I loved soccer, when everything was on the line and words could never truly express what was going on or how you were feeling. To me, soccer is poetry in motion; the words are made by the details of the game. There are so many different formations, talent strategies, and approaches to playing. No two games can ever be alike; these factors and decisions can change everything, each one creating a new stance.

The adrenaline that I had experienced earlier hummed through me once more. I clenched my fist as I felt sweat sink into the tape that was wrapped tightly around my fingers. My breathing sped up, and I tried to focus on taking steady breaths. The seconds always seemed to go by so slow when I was waiting for a player to strike from the penalty line because it was just me, them, and the ball. I think I knew when she was going to make her move even before she did. I always knew the moment when it was going to happen because it would be the moment that I would see her brace her body and draw back her leg. Once her foot connected with the ball, I listen to my body, letting my instincts take over, and I dove for the ball. I didn't even realize I had caught the ball until my fellow teammates mobbed me.

The referee blew his whistle three times, signaling the end of the game. *We won!* My inner thoughts screamed, and I didn't think this moment could get any better till I was nudged by Simone.

"Looks like you have an admirer." She chuckled. I followed her gaze toward the bleachers where I spotted Dean holding up a sign that read "I Love the Goalie." Well, I guess I was wrong; this moment did just get a whole lot better.

After the game, Dean didn't reveal to us where we were going for dinner until we got to our destination.

"Oh my god, I love this restaurant!" my mom squealed as we pulled up a place called Joe's Crab Shack. On the outside of the restaurant, it looked like a shack that you might find on a beach, which fit their surf and turf menu.

Now I knew Dean had some plan because Dean hated seafood. That's when he came up behind me and whispered, "I brought us here because it's your mom's favorite restaurant. Like I said, I have a plan."

"But why are you trying so hard to please her? How does that fit into your plan?" I asked, trying to sound understanding, but I just couldn't understand how this would help his plan. My mom never liked him, yet he still tried so hard to get on her good side. I felt as though she didn't deserve his incredible kindness; I could see her darkness, and I didn't want it to hurt him like it had hurt me.

"Just wait and see, sweetie," he said as he left my side, leaving his warmness on my ear. I didn't want to wait and see. I wanted to know what was going on now. I trusted Dean, but it was the not knowing that I hated the most.

Dean always knew how to make me happy, and even though we were out having dinner with my family, we were in our own little world. My dinner came with two crab legs, and I was having too much fun with them. I grabbed the connected tendon and was making the crab legs do the can-can. Dean and I found this so funny we couldn't stop laughing. It took a good fifteen minutes for us to gather ourselves.

"So, Helga, how was the dinner?" Dean asked.

"It was great," my mother replied, wiping the remains of any food off her face.

"I just wanted to take you all out to dinner tonight because it is Hailey's and Mr. Wyatt's birthday, but I know you guys also have a long day of moving tomorrow," Dean said, sounding extremely polite.

Oh, crap, my inner voice cursed. I had entirely forgotten about the move tomorrow. I didn't own much, so I had started packing the day my mom told me we were moving, which meant I didn't have that much more to pack.

I honestly couldn't wait till we moved because we were currently living with one of my mother's friends again. I was sharing a room with my brother, and my mom's friend was worse than she was. She was convinced that I was having sex all the time and that I always snuck my boyfriend into the house in the middle of the night. I tried to sit down with her one day and explain to her that I didn't want to have sex before I was married, that Dean respected that, but she never wanted to listen. Having one overbearing, mean women in my life was already one too many. So it wasn't a bad thing that we were moving; it was in my opinion a really good thing. Not only was my current home a bad living situation, where we lived right now was a very long distance away from where Dean lived. It would take Dean almost an hour to drive and come get me. This is because I practically live on the opposite side of town. Now our new place would only be a few minutes from Dean's house. I was so happy that we were going to live closer to each other, and I could barely contain my excitement.

"So do you need an extra hand for moving tomorrow?" Dean asked, continuing the conversation about the move. "We could use my Jeep and my dad's trailer if you would like."

Was this also part of Dean's plan? Was he trying to get my mother to warm up to him? Was his big plan to get my mom to let him help us to move? If so, he could have saved himself time and money because all he had to do was just ask her. She would have said yes because if Dean helped us to move, that meant less work and moving that she had to do.

"That would be very nice, Dean," my mother said, once again happy with the fact that she was getting something free, this time it being free labor.

The next day was of course moving day, and I woke up to Dean slowly coaxing me awake. I slowly pried open my eyes to see Dean holding in one hand a Starbucks and in the other side a box of donuts. God, he was my hero. I climbed out of bed, and when he placed the coffee and donuts down, I ran into his arms. When I hugged him, I didn't want to let go. Even though I just saw him, it felt like it had been forever. When we hugged, his smell always seemed to punch through my senses, and I couldn't help but love the way he smelled. To me, he smelled like the outdoors right when the morning sun just rose. He smelled like pure sexiness; he smelled like safety, and the best part is he smelled like forever. It was becoming very clear to me that I was starting to crave the way he smelled, and only his scent would calm me like this.

"So, Mrs. Wyatt, what's first?" Dean asked my mother shortly after I had finally let him go, and we had made our way downstairs.

"The big stuff, then the boxes," she replied without even saying "good morning" to me first.

"You guys are so lucky to be getting this new big place. I wish I could get out of my parents' house," Dean stated, sounding a little sad.

That's weird, I thought. Dean loved his parents, and he loved being with his parents; and as far as I knew, they hadn't been pressuring him to move out either since he was only nineteen. Dean's parents liked having a big house full of loud kids. Dean's mom once told me that if she had it her way, as long as her kids did what they were supposed to do, she would let them live there as long as they wanted.

The day seemed to have dragged on and on, most likely because I had forgotten how much work moving was. Dean however was like a one-man moving team, and for every one load I took, he took two.

As the sun started to set, the sweat from my forehead started to feel more like someone had placed a wet, cold washrag on my head. Throughout the whole day, Dean and my mother talked about how Dean wanted freedom and how he wanted to be on his own, that he wanted to have bills and responsibilities and all I could keep thinking was, *No one wants any of that.*

Eventually I tuned out their conversation because trying to figure out Dean's angle was only giving me a headache. I didn't tune back in until a single shocking comment left my mother's mouth that I never thought would be said in a million years. "Hey, Dean, I have an idea, and I don't know why I didn't think of it sooner. Why don't you move in with us?"

That's when both my head and Dean's snapped up, giving Helga our full attention.

"I wouldn't want to inconvenience you all," Dean responded.

"You would be doing no such thing. You could share a room with Ross, and of course, you'll have to pay rent. It would be like having a place of your own but with roommates," my mother bargained.

Now, my mom's bizarre offer made sense. I knew there had to be a reason why she was so eager to have Dean move in. With him paying rent,, she would have more money to spend. Why couldn't my mother ever do anything out of the kindness of her heart?

Before Dean could turn down, accept, or further discuss my mom's offer, Ross cried out, "But I don't want to share my room with anyone!"

My mother and brother argued for nearly two hours about Ross and Dean sharing a room. Ross kept stating that he was looking forward to his own room and that he was tired of always sharing, which I could understand because he was a teenage boy, and I too felt the same, but he looked up to Dean; he practically worshiped him. I knew my mother wouldn't let Ross win this agreement because Dean paying a portion of the rent meant too much to my mom. By the two-hour mark, my mother finally came walking back over toward where Dean and I were sitting.

"So here's the deal," my mom fumed in a semi-rude manner, causing Dean to remove his arm that was draped over my shoulders. "Melvin and I have decided that because Ross is throwing a fit about sharing his room, Dean and Hailey, you both may share a room together." She eyed us both. This must be a dream I thought as I pinched myself realizing that I was still awake.

"Wait, what?" I finally blurted out, trying not to stare opened-mouth at my mom.

"But there are rules you two must follow a hundred percent if you want this to happen," Helga made known. She continued when she saw us both nod our heads in agreement. "You two are to sleep in separate beds. You are not allowed to dress in front of each other ever, and the door to your bedroom will be open at all times!" My mother counted the rules off like she was a drill sergeant, and we were new recruits.

"Are you sure you're okay with me sharing a room with Hailey, Mrs. Wyatt? I wouldn't want to disrespect you, your home, or your family in anyway." Dean commented, sounding serious, but I could see that he was trying hard not to smile. I was trying to stop my eyes from bulging out of my head. I couldn't believe that any of this was happening.

"As long as you two follow all of my rules, you will not be disrespecting me," my mother cautioned.

Later that night, after everything was said and done, we had finally moved everything into the new place. Dean decided to drive back to his parent's house to tell them about his plans to move in with me and my family. Before he left, I had to ask him the one question that I had been dying to ask since my mom's living arrangements idea. "Baby, before you go, can I ask you a question?" I asked as I stepped in front of him.

"You know you can always ask me anything," he replied as he started tracing circles on my upper arm.

"Was this your big plan? To move in with us?" I asked, bringing my voice down to a whisper so we wouldn't be overheard.

"Actually, yes!" he stated firmly. "I have this overwhelming need to protect you. Every time we are away I feel like there is a piece of me missing. Then when I see you again, I am whole. But I look in your eyes, and I see that a little bit of you breaks anytime that woman is around you," he continued, and I stood there speechless, so he continued. "I need to protect you, keep you safe anyway I can. Living with your family was going to help me ensure that. It only could work if your mother thought it was her idea. She would have never let me move in if I had asked. However, I never imagined actually sharing a room with you, but that's just even better. Now I can guarantee your safety." He finished.

"How did you know?" I whispered, awed that he could see something that no one else ever could.

"You're the other half of me. I don't know how to explain it. I just know. It's like a sixth sense. I call it 'Hailey sonar,'" he stated before winking at me. Before I could say more, Dean yanked me to him, crushing his mouth to mine, and a tiny moan left my lips as I lost the ability to breathe. I became lost in the fabric of time as his finger wrapped themselves into my hair. I held on to the back of his shirt as tight as I could until I finally pulled away.

"You should go. It wouldn't do us any good at all if my mom saw us kiss like that!" I exclaimed with a shaky breathe.

After a few more stolen kisses, Dean finally headed to his parents' house, and shortly after, my phone alerted me. I was so distracted by unpacking that I didn't even bother to check the caller ID. I answered the phone with a chipper "Hello."

"Yes, hello is this Hailey?" asked the unknown woman.

"Yes, this is her," I replied puzzled.

"I'm sorry to have disturbed you so late, but this is Mrs. Heart," Dean's mom said politely.

"How are you?" I asked, now nervous about the reason for her call.

"I'm doing great, thank you for asking. My reason for this call is I just finished talking to Dean, and he seems pretty determined to live with you, and he is an adult, so I cannot stop him. He is currently packing his belongings, and I wanted to make him a sandwich to go but can't seem to remember at this moment what he likes on his sandwich. Do you happen to know?" she rambled on.

Did she call me just to ask me how Dean likes his sandwiches? Did she hate me for being the reason her son was moving out? Not wanting her to wait while I took too much time trying to understand her question, I answered her with how much I knew about how Dean liked his sandwich. "He likes white bread. Turkey is his favorite sandwich meat, and he hates onions and mayonnaise. So just put mustard and pickles with either American or Swiss cheese, he likes both."

It took a few moments for her to reply. "That's correct," she said, sounding a little surprised.

Did she want me to be wrong? Was she expecting me to be wrong? Was this some kind of test? I instantly flashed back to the first day I met Dean and couldn't help but to smile. What was up with that family and their personal test?

"Can I ask for one favor before we hang up, Hailey?" she asked, now sounding more serious.

"Of course, anything," I said, waiting for her favor.

"Take care of my son," she stated.

"I will, forever, if he lets me," I said, meaning every word, and then there was silence, and I knew she had hung up.

CHAPTER 5

Polar Bears

Sometimes you will never know the value of a
moment until it becomes a memory.
—Dr. Seuss

Though a month had already passed, the greatest feeling in the world was waking up and looking into the two bluest eyes that looked like shattered marbles. Those eyes knew me to my deepest core. They knew all my secrets and all my fears. For the first time, I could say that I loved with everything I had and I was truly loved in return. This love was playful, beautiful, and unexpected. It was never judging, and it was never hateful. It was pure, and it was innocent. This love was Dean.

"Good morning," his voice sang like angels, and it settled into my soul.

"Good morning, sexy," I said, unable to stop myself from smiling like a fool.

"How did you sleep?" he asked, rubbing away the drowsiness from his eyes. His voice was still thick with sleep, but I knew he was awake enough to remember the conversation we were having.

"Good actually!" I murmured as I stretched like a cat.

"Great, well get up and get dressed. We have plans today, sweetheart." A toying smile tugged at his face as he got out of our bed.

Even though my mom had stated that we sleep in separate beds, we found out we got better sleep when we slept in the same bed. It's not like we did anything inappropriate because Dean respected my "no sex before marriage" rule. Also, we made sure my mother never found out by not getting in the same bed till after she went to sleep and getting out of bed before she woke up. I know that in a way, it was bad, but I felt that I deserved the happiness that Dean gives me.

"Where are we going?" I shrieked as I jumped out of bed, unable to contain my excitement.

"It's a surprise." He laughed, taking off his shirt and distracting me for a brief moment. He sometimes made this abstinence rule so hard, and I was a teenage girl with an extremely attractive boyfriend.

"Come on, please tell me," I begged.

"It wouldn't be a surprise if I told you," he joked.

The whole car ride to our destination, he made me keep my eyes closed. I tried my hardest to listen for any clues about my surroundings to try and figure our destination. I heard nothing but the noise coming from inside the car. I heard the car engine humming, and The Used song "Smother Me" was playing on the radio. When the car finally came to a stop, I heard the engine make a clicking sound as it cut off.

"Okay, open your eyes," he said, and I finally removed my hands, letting light flood into my now sensitive eyes. It took a moment for my eyes to adjust, but once they did, I knew exactly where we were.

"The zoo?" I asked. "What are we doing here?" I spoke, hoping that I didn't come off as rude, but my curiosity was overtaking me yet again.

"Yes, the zoo. I thought you might like to come here. I remember you saying that you hadn't been here in a while."

Even though it felt a little childish, he was right. I was excited because I hadn't been to the zoo in a very long time. The last time I was at the zoo, I was six, and I went because my grandmother had taken me. The only reason why I remember going at such a young age was because I ended up sitting on a cactus, and my grandmother had to pull needles out of my butt. That was something that was very hard to forget. This time, I was going to make sure I looked where I was sitting before I sat down.

I was jubilant that he remembered and wanted to take me. All I knew was we could have gone anywhere, and I would have been happy no matter what as long as he was there. He came around to my side and opened the door for me. Before I could step out, he reached into the cab of the car to grab my hand. His fingers clasped through mine, and they fit perfectly together like puzzle pieces, like we were made for one another.

Then just like that, my day bright day faded to gray.

"Hey, Dean, thanks for inviting me!"

The shrill voice I have come to dread rang out. There, my mother stood at the entrance to the zoo with a smile that looked awfully fake plastered on her face.

My grip tightened on Dean's hand as I pulled him down to my level, and I hissed in his ear, "What is going on?"

"I invited her," he stated, and my mouth dropped open.

"What? Why?" I stuttered.

"You'll see. It's all part of my plan." He winked.

Wait, his plan wasn't just to move in? What more could he want now? Only he would have multiple parts to his overall plan. I thought and couldn't help but laugh as I loosened my grip and followed him with faith, knowing that he had a good plan. My mother happened to have an unwanted effect on me, and I couldn't help but tense up whenever she was near.

The whole time we walked at the zoo, I racked my brain, trying to figure out why he had invited her. She was always against us, and we barely had time to ourselves as it was, even less than before he had moved in. My mother figured that we didn't need to go out because we lived together, and when we were home, my mom always had us doing something for her. Even so, in the end, it was all worth it because every morning I got to wake up to him, and I really hope that he felt the same.

I tried to shake off the anxiety feeling that drifted over me and tried to enjoy Dean's company. I kept reassuring myself that Dean had a plan last time, and it worked, so maybe this one will work too.

Dean stopped in his tracks and turned to face me. "I'll be right back. I have to take care of something." And with a kiss on my forehead, he trotted toward my mom. "Excuse me, Helga. Can I steal a minute of your time?" Dean asked politely.

"Sure, buddy," she replied, following Dean.

Fifteen minutes had gone by, but it felt like an eternity, and then my mother and Dean finally emerged from behind the corner they disappeared around a few moments ago. Dean slid his arm around me.

"Take a walk with me," he whispered in my ear, and I looked up at him to find him grinning.

I looked over at my mom to see if she was going to follow, and it wasn't until she said, "Go ahead," with tears in her eyes that I realized she was staying behind.

Was she really crying? What did Dean say to make her cry? What was going on? My mind screamed in panic. I hadn't seen this much emotion in my mother in a long time.

"Relax, I can tell you're panic-thinking again," Dean reassured as he tightened his grip on me. I instantly relaxed, trusting him, as I always had and always will because I felt safe with him. We followed a narrow path that went down a small paved hill. I discovered it was a lower observatory area for the polar bears. It was constructed to look like a cave, and the water from the polar bear tank cast a blue light around the cave, lighting it in a beautiful earthy-type light.

I looked in the animal exhibit and saw two beautiful playful polar bears splashing and playing with each other.

"Wow, look at them," I said in wonderment.

No reply came from Dean; instead, he gently put his fingers under my chin to pull my gaze toward him.

"Can I ask you a question?" Dean asked with a serious look on his face.

A rush of panic went through me "Of course, you know you can ask me anything," I replied, my heart thudding in my chest.

Then Dean dropped to his knee, and my heart leaped and raced. I was afraid it would pound out of my chest. And like a total cliché, I place my hand over my heart.

"I love you. Will you marry me?" Dean asked nervously.

I didn't even take a second longer to think because I always knew the answer. "Yes!" I shrieked, and he stood up so I could leap into his arms. He cradled my face between the palms of his hands and began to gently kiss me in a way that drove me crazy. What had started off soft and tender soon grew into more as we alternated between nibbling on each other's lips and open-mouth probing with our tongues. Dean hands went into my hair, gripping it in order to pull me tighter into him. He kissed me hard, and the kiss was passionately erotic and fierce,, making my heart stutter again. I knew at that moment that I was committing myself to Dean forever, and being his wife felt so right.

"I'm sorry I don't have a ring for you, but I promise I will get you one soon. I want to save up for the perfect one for you," Dean whispered against my lips, sounding a little ashamed.

I didn't want him to feel like that, so I answered him the only way I knew how, from my heart. "I don't care about rings, and I don't even need one. I'll marry you anytime and anyplace. You don't need to get me a ring to make me yours. I've been yours already for a long time," I said, pulling him to me so I can kiss him again.

He pulled away quickly, so I could see the huge smile on his face. "I am happy you said that. I am going to get you a ring one day, but for now I got you this." Dean smiled, reaching into his pocket. The first thing I could see was a silver chain, and it wasn't until Dean held it up in front of me that I was able to see that there was a charm.

"Is that a polar bear?" I asked with a goofy smile on my face.

"Yes, I thought it was appropriate," he answered as he fastened the necklace around my neck.

"What would you have done if I said no?" I asked as I touched the charm that now hung around my neck.

"I knew you wouldn't. You can't live without me any more than I can live without you," he whispered before kissing me yet again.

We left the zoo later that day, and I felt the happiest I ever had in my entire life, and my heart felt like it had mended a little more that day.

Even though I had already said yes to Dean the first time he asked me to marry him, he continued to ask me almost every single day. I don't know if he was afraid I would change my mind, or he thought it was all a dream, but I in no way minded it because whenever he asked, I still felt heat rise to my cheeks, and my heart would race every time. The most surprising part of it all was that he found a new way to ask me every time. I hoped this happiness never ended because now that I knew this kind of love, not having it would destroy me.

Dean saved me in every possible way. He stopped the growing darkness from spreading inside me with the love he gave me. He kept me strong, and he made me believe in my dreams again. He made me want things I never knew I wanted. He made me want kids, and he made me want to grow old with him. I knew that what I felt for him wasn't just a stupid crush. It hadn't been that for a long time, and there would be no one else in this world that could replace Dean.

Without him, I would be nothing; with him, I was everything I never knew I could be.

Dean one day went on to do the most respectable thing someone with the intent of marriage could do. He asked my father's permission for my hand in marriage. That action made me fall even more in love with him, which I didn't think was possible. He even surprised my father because as my father said, "I didn't know men still did that."

One of the best qualities about Dean that I loved was how he was new-fashioned and old-fashioned all at the same time. He had ideals and beliefs that he stuck to, and he believed in having respect for someone you loved. He would always open the doors for me and pull out my chair when I went to sit at a table. He was going to be mine forever; he was my modern-day knight, my very own miracle. In my heart, I knew that if we ever had a daughter, I wanted her to find someone just like her father. Someone who respected her and treated her in a manner that every man should.

With all this happiness, I should have seen what happened next coming because when I thought I had everything in my life under control, my life would throw a new unexpected challenge at me.

CHAPTER 6

Trouble Begins

*People who have trouble questioning their own country
often have trouble admitting fault in themselves, both of
which come from insecurity and lack of humility.*
—Bryant Mcgill.

"Get dressed. We were invited over to my friend's house for dinner," my mother demanded as she popped her head into my room.

"Do I have to go? I kind of have plans with Dean," I replied, sounding like I felt, reluctant and not wanting to go. I crossed my fingers behind my back, hoping she would take the hint and say I didn't have to go.

"You guys are getting married, and you live with each other. One day apart isn't going to kill you two. Now let's go!" she stated, her tone having authority in it. Along dreadful sigh escaped through my lips.

In the car, I texted Dean to let him know what was going on because he had gone to work that afternoon. I told him how he missed the scene of my mom dragging me out of the house, practically kicking and screaming on the way out like a five-year-old.

"Sorry, baby, we have to cancel our plans today. Helga is making me go over to her friend's house with her for dinner. Rain check?"

As always, I received his response within minutes. "Your mom has friends? Lol. Just kidding but what friend?"

I had no idea because my mother wouldn't tell me, but before I could respond, we pulled into the entrance of an apartment complex. A few moments later, our car pulled into a parking space next to a van that looked terribly familiar, but for some reason, I couldn't remember it.

"Helga, over here," a voice called out from nowhere, and I followed the voice, looking toward the direction it came from, and my blood ran cold. It then hit me why that van looked so familiar because standing there waving at my mom was my ex-boyfriend Troy. Which meant dinner was at his house, and it wasn't going to be a pleasant reunion.

I sent a quick text to Dean telling him of the new details that have just unfolded. "Dean, I need help. My mom took me to dinner at Troy's house!" I typed, a little panicky.

A minute later, a text popped up on my phone, and as I read, the four trivial words he sent me instantly calmed me: "I'm on my way."

The history of Troy and me wasn't a very pleasant one. He and I dated a brief time back when I was about fifteen going on sixteen. He was much older than me by almost ten years. It was a relationship I was forced into by my mother. It all started one day when my sister had her first child and decided to cut our mom out of her life. This of course made my mom want to go to the extremes. One day, my mom took me out for a drive, and I could just tell she wanted to ask me something.

"What is it, Mom? Come out with it already," I said, wanting to know what she wanted.

"I wanted to know how you felt about artificial insemination," she had asked, and I looked at her with an open mouth.

"Um, if I were thirty and had no husband, I would consider it. Or if I couldn't have children or my husband couldn't give me any or if I had a same-sex partner. Does this have something to do with Agatha keeping the baby away from you?" I speculated, still in complete shock.

"What, no I am so over your sister. She broke my heart and kept me away from my granddaughter. I'll never forgive her for what she did to me," my mom complained.

My sister didn't do anything to my mom, even though my mom has convinced herself that my sister did wrong her in some way. My sister did the same thing I planned on doing when I turned eighteen: put my foot down and no longer let me mother walk all over me. It was what my sister did when she decided to marry someone my mom didn't want her to marry. My sister just had her first kid and still hadn't let our mother see the baby. I honestly don't know why my mother expected better treatment when she treated someone horribly; eventually they aren't going to stay around to let you continuously do it.

When I sat there in silence, my mom continued, "Well, you know you can always get the insemination and give me the baby… "

"What! No, Mother. If I was ever to have a child, that child would be mine, no one else's," I shouted, looking away from my mother, trying to stop myself from shaking from all my anger. "Do me a favor, Mother. Don't ever suggest anything like that to me again. I will never bring an innocent child into this world so that you can make Agatha jealous."

A few days after we had that conversation, Troy asked me out. Troy was the oldest son of my mother's best friend. He was almost ten years older than I was. My mom bugged me for days, telling me to give him a shot, and just so she would stop, I said yes. Dating him, for me, was uncomfortable because he only wanted one thing from me, sex. About two weeks into our relationship, I walked into the house and found Troy's mom and my mother waiting for me.

"Is this an intervention?" I joked, dropping my book bag onto the floor.

"This is no time for jokes, Hailey. I am going to ask you to please take the conversation we are about to have with you seriously," my mother said sternly.

"Okay, what's going on?" I asked, sitting in a chair across from them.

"Well, one of Troy's ex-girlfriends found out you two were dating, and she found out how old you are," she brought forth. I couldn't help but think that no one would have found out that we were dating if these two women I was looking at didn't go around bragging about it. How did I know this? It was because I know I wasn't the one going around bragging about it.

"Okay, I'm failing to see the problem here," I said, clearly amused.

"Well, because of your age and his, it's against the law for you two to date." My mother paused, waiting for my reaction, and I tried hard to hide my smile.

"Well… " I began, trying to not sound too happy, but before I could finish my sentence, I was interrupted.

"Your mother and I decided that it would be best if you two got married," Troy's mom blurted out.

"Um, what?" I stuttered confused. "I barely know him, and we only just started dating," I stated, explicitly refusing the offer.

"We understand if you need time to think about it," my mother commented, and I realized that nothing I said would make them understand that I did not want to marry Troy. So I answered the only way I could.

"Yeah, sure, I'll think about it."

The adults let out a girlish squeal and then started talking wedding plans and the future. I began to walk upstairs and didn't let my smile show until I was out of sight. I just bought enough time to speak with Troy and tell him how crazy this was.

When I finally did get to talk with Troy, it didn't go well at all.

"Hey, my future missus," he said with a real smile on his face.

Crap, his mother got to him first. As he came up to me for a hug, I put my hand out to stop him. "We need to talk," I said, feeling a little bad about what I was about to do. We found a quiet room, and I looked at him and got straight to the point.

"I'm sorry if you were told I said yes, but I didn't, and I'm sorry, but I can't marry you."

He stood there in silence, and I watched as he went from stunned to angry, just proving why we would never work. I could never be with someone who couldn't talk to me about my feelings or concern. A relationship must always be a partnership, and you should never get mad at someone because you do like how they feel.

"And why not?" Troy raised his voiced and clenched his hands into a fist.

I stood my ground and made my case. "Can't you see that you and I would never work? And I'm sorry, but I could never love you."

"Oh, because you're so much better than me, aren't you!" Troy exploded with cruelty.

"No, but I would never date someone who does illegal drugs and drinks to the point of passing out. Are you saying you're willing to give those things up for me?" I asked, already knowing his answer.

"No… you're not worth it!" Troy declared, clearly trying to hurt me.

"Well, then I guess we have nothing left to discuss." I left and hadn't spoken to him since. It wasn't until later that I found out the true reason why my mother wanted us to date. He and my sister went out for a short period of time. She probably figured that if it didn't work out with one daughter, she always had another. In the end, my mother of course was not happy at all, but I didn't give her a choice, and because I was the only daughter left that still talked to her, she had no choice but to give up on it, or at least I thought she had.

I blinked fast, startled at how seeing someone could bring back a flood of awful memories. When we exited the car, I pulled my mom to the side with a hard jerk of her arm. Believe me, I got her full attention then. "What the hell are we doing here?" I hissed, letting her know that I was clearly pissed off. She knew what had happened with Troy, yet she still brought me here.

"We were invited. That's what we are doing here," my mom replied, and I could tell that she thought she had outsmarted me. She thought that I thought she had no part in this dinner party.

"I don't want to be here, Mother. I'm not okay with this," I whispered, trying not to sound helpless.

"I don't care what you want, and these are my friends, and you're my daughter. I have a say over you until you're eighteen," she said with a smirk on her face, knowing she had won this argument.

"Okay, fine!" I smiled at my mother, making her expression go from victory to confusion. She turned and started to walk away, and before she opened the house door, I called out, "Oh, by the way, Dean is on his way."

My mom stopped for a brief moment as her hands tightened on the doorknob, causing her knuckles to turn white. With nothing to say, she opened the door and walked inside.

The heat beat down on me as I met Dean on the blacktop of the apartment complex's basketball court. Today he was wearing a pair of blue jeans and a red long-sleeve plaid shirt. He had the sleeves rolled up on both arms just past his elbows. Once our eyes met, his face lit up, and his million-dollar smile showed. There was that smile again; it always made me go weak in the knees, but before I could hug him, he gripped my shoulders, and he pulled me into his arms. The air rushed out of my lungs as he tilted my head back so he could kiss me. This kiss was different than the others we had shared; it was firm, and I felt it all the way to my bones. It seemed as if he was claiming my very soul, and I know he left this invisible brand on my heart. I could feel all his emotions and thoughts in his kiss. I could feel my heart and soul being anchored down. My body melted into his, completely forgetting where we were until the sound of someone clearing his throat came from behind us. We reluctantly broke apart in order to turn toward the noise as both of us tried to steady our breathing. Before any introductions could be made, the man had walked up behind us and introduced himself.

"You must be Dean. I'm Troy."

Dean smiled down at me and kissed me on the forehead before he proceeded to walk toward Troy. With his hand extended, Dean shook Troy's hand.

"It's nice to meet you. Hailey has told me a lot about you."

"I bet they were all good things," said Troy, winking at me. Dean's gaze stayed the same, and if Troy was trying to make Dean mad or jealous, it apparently wasn't working.

Then out of nowhere, my little brother, Ross, popped up from behind Troy. My brother was only a year younger than me, and unfortunately, he didn't have a mind for himself. He didn't have a mind for himself because he spent most of his time trying to look cool and following those he idolized instead of being his own person. He was smart and sweet but tended to get himself in a lot of trouble by doing what others told him to do. The worst part of all is he let my mother control him in every way; he did everything she said, no matter what.

"Hey, guys. Hey, Dean, Troy and I were about to shoot some hoops. Want to join?" Ross asked.

I was about to decline when Dean's voice chimed in, "Sure."

Well, this wasn't going to end well.

As we took our spots on the court, I couldn't help but to look back and forth between Dean and Troy, who have yet to look away from each other. Right before the game could even start, Troy took his shirt off, exposing his skinny body structure. I could see Dean trying not to laugh as the game began. As the game went on, Troy started to talk about the relationship he and I used to have, if you could even call it that, how good we were together and how he had me first. But no matter how hard Troy tried, he couldn't get a rise out of Dean. I could tell Troy was trying to start a fight, and he reminded me a little of a dog trying to mark his territory. Still, Dean didn't get upset and seemed to be very calm. Dean got possession of the ball and dribbled the ball, and then without hesitation, he shot it. *Swish* was all we heard, and the ball went into the net.

"Well, she is with me now," he said as he reached for my hand. His fingers interlaced with mine, and just like every time, a perfect fit.

Weeks passed, and my mom never said or brought up what happened that day, probably because she knew I was still upset about it. Today, Dean had to work so my mom had to come and pick me up from school.

"How was school?" she greeted me as I entered the car.

"It was good. Finished all my homework in my free period today," I answered. We sat in silence for a while, and then my mom broke the ice.

"So I decided that I don't like Dean's mother and sister."

I turned my head and looked at my mom and hope she saw the anger in my eyes.

CHAPTER 7

The Purple Dress

After you're dead and buried and floating around whatever place we go to, what's going to be your best memory of earth? What one moment for you defines what it's like to be alive on this planet?
—Douglas Coupland

"Don't look at me like that, Hailey. I am only expressing my opinion," my mother yelled as if she had said nothing wrong and in no way deserved my anger toward her.

"This should be good," I said. "Why do you not like Constantine and Mable?"

"Well, frankly, I don't like Dean's mom. Constantine runs her house like a whorehouse," my mom criticized.

"What? No, she does not," I exclaimed, totally appalled.

"She lets her kids have sex in her house!" she barked.

"The way she thinks is that her kids are going to have sex no matter what, and at least if it's under her roof, she can make sure they are safe. I think that she is their mother and an adult, and she can set whatever rules she wants for her kids. We are also in no place to make judgment on her or her views and beliefs," I debated. I thought I had made some solid points and that she would take back her comments. I clearly thought wrong.

"Well, I'm entitled to my opinion, and that's how I feel," she declared.

"You are right. You are entitled to your opinion, everyone is, but you don't need to be rude while expressing your opinion," I suggested.

"Well, don't you want to hear why I don't like Dean's sister, Mable?" my mother continued.

"Not really because I have a feeling it's not going to be nice, and I didn't ask because I knew you were going to tell me anyway," I muttered.

"She is a bitch!" she exclaimed.

"Helga!" I screamed, now outraged.

"Well, she is. Last time I was over, I said hi, and she completely ignored me," she replied, sounding conceded.

Sweat began forming on my brow, not because the car was hot but for the lone fact of all the rage that was building up inside. I was shaking with anger and trying not to explode; it wouldn't be good if I did. "Well, for your information, Mother, Mable has a social issue. She doesn't talk to people she doesn't know. It took her almost a year to say something to me, and I'm dating her brother," I comforted.

"Well, that's my opinion, and that's how I feel," Helga responded.

"Okay, and again, thank you for always sharing your opinion, but have you ever cared or thought about how your comments make Dean feel? How what you say can hurt other people. Words cut a lot deeper than any knife ever could. How do you think Dean would feel when you sit here and talk bad about his family?" I coaxed.

What came out of her mouth next shouldn't have surprised me, but like always, she managed to find a way. No matter how many times I've heard my mother say hurtful things or do hurtful things, in the end, I'm still always shocked. I can't imagine, and I can't under-stand why someone would choose to be so mean and vindictive. I also never could understand how I could come from someone who had so much hatred in her heart, but like I said, I was always still floored when I heard how she felt.

"No, I don't care. This is how I feel, and if he has such a problem with it, then he can get the fuck out of my house. And if you have a problem with my opinion as well, he can take you with him!" she exploded.

As soon as she finished, everything in me stilled, and all that anger that was in me just a few moments ago making me shake with rage disappeared. And strangely, I felt at peace as if I was waiting my entire life to know how my mother felt about me, how much she valued me as a daughter, and now I knew. I meant so little to her that she would actually discard me. She would throw me away just because her opinion was wrong and just because I stood up for what was right. She would rather have children who follow her mindlessly. If they weren't, then she didn't want them at all. She was mad because I wasn't falling in step to her side and doing everything she said. I knew what I had to do next.

"Okay, Mom, you can have it your way. But when I'm no longer in your life, you'll only have yourself to blame," my voice cracked.

My hand grabbed the car's door handle. I paused for only a second to see if she was going to stop me and apologize for everything she said, but deep down, I knew she wasn't going to stop me. I threw the car door open and grabbed my backpack off the floor and did both of these actions in an angry manner, only because I wanted her to know that I was pissed and that I would never forgive her for this, ever. I climbed out of the car and slammed my door, heading off toward the one place I used to run to where I felt safe before Dean had come into my life.

I exited the parking lot that was located directly across from my high school and started walking down the street. Five minutes turned into ten, and I had just reached the chained link fence that encased the lush green field that I played on, the field I put all my sweat and tears on. Because of all my time I spent on this field, I had discovered a break in the fence where I could climb through. Before I climbed through the fence this time, I turned and looked back one last time to see if my mother had followed. I wasn't surprised to see the streets empty; it was then that I promised myself that I would never look back again. I ducked through the hole and walked toward the soccer field.

I walked up to the goal and ran my fingers over the metal letting the smoothness settle in my soul calming my chaotic emotions. I threw my backpack on the ground and followed suit. I laid flat on the soft grass and used my backpack as a pillow. I pulled out my cell phone and made a crucial phone call to the one person I loved. It calmed me more than soccer ever could. As always, he answered the phone after only a couple rings.

"Hey, baby, everything okay?" he asked with a soothing voice.

"Yeah, sorry to bother you at work, but we might not have a place to live anymore," I replied, staying calm.

"What happened?" Dean asked, sounding confused.

"Helga went on one of her rants again about your family. I asked her to stop for your sake, and she of course said no and told me that if you and I didn't like it, we could leave." I laughed, finding the whole situation now funny.

"Are you okay? Where are you?" Dean asked, and before I could answer, I heard him tell his supervisor that he had a family emergency come up and had to go. Hearing him call me family made my crumbling world whole again. I could tell he was holding his breath now, awaiting my reply.

"Yes, I'm fine. I walked out of the car and came to the place where you told everyone you loved me." I smiled.

"Okay, I'll be there soon, and don't worry, baby, we will figure something out. I love you," he reassured.

"I love you too, baby," I replied and then pushed the End button on my phone, ending the phone call on a sweet note.

I laid there and let my emotions run through me, and even though I was upset, no tears seemed to come, even though a part of me was devastated, knowing that my mother didn't love me enough to change, that I wasn't good enough to love. Over the years, she had broken me so bad and made me shed so many tears that there were none left to fall now. The other half of me was relieved because I now could be the real me, and I no longer had to jump through hoops to win my mother's love and to be able to have her be proud of me. That never happened, and now it never would. I had however found someone who loved me for me.

I laid there for a little while longer until I finally realized that I couldn't stay because Dean was going to be arriving outside the school any minute. I made quick haste, collecting my bag and ducking through the hole in the fence again. Then I broke out into a run and followed the same path as earlier, and the walk that took me ten minutes now only took me a few minutes. As I rounded the last corner, I saw him, still in his work uniform. He was leaning against his Jeep, and I could tell he was lost in thought. As if he knew I was there, he turned so his eyes connected with mine. It felt as if electricity was coursing through us, and I could tell he sensed it too because he gave me his famous full wattage smile that always made me melt in the knees. I broke out into another run, letting my bag fall to the floor right before I reached him, and I flung myself into his arms. Him holding me made me feel whole again, and realizing at that moment that without him I am broken made me break down. A tiny sob escaped me, and I tried to hide it in his clothing and shoulder, but I know he still heard it.

"Shhhh, baby, it's okay. We are going to be fine," he soothed. I tried to calm myself down so I could reply, but he went on. "I'm so sorry that you're crying because of me. You didn't have to protect me.

If you want, we can go to your mom's house and ask for forgiveness," he said, sounding sincere.

"Don't be silly," I choked out. "I'm not crying because I'm sad about my mother. I know this doesn't make any sense, but I'm crying because I'm happy. It took all that happened and this moment for me to realize that I'm so happy and lucky to have met you. I feel complete, and I've never loved anyone as much as I love you," I added shyly.

"I love you too, baby, and I'll give you the life you deserve, even if it takes everything I have." He breathed as he leaned in close, capturing my lips. Even though we've kissed many times before, this kiss was different, more intense.

I opened my mouth wider in order to give him better access as we deepened our kiss unable to stop ourselves. Dean turned me around slowly in order to press me up against the Jeep. He pressed his body against mine, trying to get as close as he could. A desperate need arose in me that I didn't know I had, and I felt his smooth hair run through my fingers. Once my fingers were fully in his hair, I grabbed hold and held him to me, trying to make him realize how much I loved him, to show him with my passion for him that I failed to be able to tell him with my words, to try and pull a piece of him inside of me, to make us closer than we already are.

When we finally pulled away from each other, it wasn't because we wanted to but for air.

"Wow!" Dean exclaimed.

"Wow!" I mimicked, pressing the tip of my fingers gently against my kiss-swollen lips.

Giving me his wolfish smile, he intertwined his fingers with mine and started to pull me toward the passenger car door.

"Come on, we have a stop to make," he informed me as he opened my door. With my mind still jumbled from the kiss, all I could do is nod in response. He traveled quickly to the driver side and climbed in and automatically intertwined our fingers once again right after he started the vehicle. As we drove to our destination, Dean continued his contact by bringing my hand to his mouth, kissing my knuckles or by nibbling on my fingers. About ten minutes later, we had arrived at Dean's parent's house.

"What are we doing here?" I asked.

"This is just part of the plan, baby," he reassured as he winked at me.

As we walked up the path walkway, I flashed back to the day when I slipped and fell in front of Dean and thought about all that happened up until now. I squeezed his hand, realizing how I would do it all again and how I would give up everything just to have him in my life.

Dean rang the doorbell, and within seconds, Constantine was at the door. After a quick once-over, I wasn't surprised when the first question she asked us was, "What's wrong?"

"Nothing too serious," he stated. "But we should talk."

"Okay, let's go to the patio," she said, stepping aside so Dean and I could come in. We followed her through the living room, then the dining room, and continued to follow her as she opened the double doors leading to the patio area. Dean and I took the seats that were placed across from Constantine. Once we had settled, Dean started to speak but was quickly cut off by his mom.

"Hold on, before you start, I have a few questions to ask of my own," she cautioned. "Is she pregnant?"

"No!" Dean replied shocked.

"Is she in trouble with the law?" she continued.

"No!" Dean shouted, seeming to be now getting upset.

Finally, as she realized we weren't in serious trouble, Constantine tried to lighten the mood. She leaned in and whispered, "Is she a prostitute?"

"What! No!" Dean laughed.

"Okay, then what's going on?" Constantine chuckled.

"Well, remember how I told you to be prepared for when Helga went off? Well, it's happened." Then Dean went on to explain the events that transpired.

"Well, that is a little bit of a problem," Constantine murmured, breaking the silence after all the information was given. "We know your mom is a bit disturbed, and I have a feeling she isn't going to take you choosing Dean very well," Constantine continued. "But the choice of what happens next is up to you two. What would you like to do, Dean?" she asked, clearly interested in how her son felt.

"Well, I've come over here many times, Mom, and told you how much I love Hailey, and I want her in my future. I've already asked her to marry me, plus I went and had Helga sign the marriage license, so legally, Hailey can already be in my care," Dean bragged.

"Wait. When did you get a marriage license signed?" Constantine said, now lost.

"It was just a few days ago," Dean started. "I took Helga out and pampered her, and then I told her I wanted her to be in all aspects of the wedding and our life. She was so excited to help with the first step, which was the marriage license. So I took her and Melvin down to the courthouse and got everything signed," Dean stated, finishing going over what had happened very quickly. "I'm sorry I didn't tell you first, Mom, but I knew I had to do whatever I could to save Hailey. Even if it meant signing a piece of paper stating that I want to spend the rest of my life with this one woman." He smiled and then turned his attention to me. "The choice is yours. I want to marry you, and I don't care when, right now, tomorrow, or ten years from now. It's always been you. It will always be you. I know that you have to make a decision, but even if you want to marry me to save yourself from your mother, I'd be happy to have you as my wife, even if it's only for a little while," he finished saying in a husky voice.

I smiled sweetly at him, this man who yet again found a new sweet way to confess his feelings to me. I suddenly became overflowed with the amazement from this ability to be able to love Dean more and more every day.

I launched myself out of my seat, gently sat myself on his lap, and placed his face between the palms of my hands. "The first time you asked me to marry you I said yes, and I meant it. I want to marry you, not for any other reason but that I love you and I want to spend the rest of my life with you. So, yes, I'll marry you today, tomorrow, and ten years from now as long as it's you, I say I do too," I said, and then I kissed him right in front of his mother. I wanted to show him even if it was with a kiss just how much I loved him.

Unfortunately, this cherished moment didn't last long. *Honk! Honk! Honk!*

"Send my daughter out here right this minute!" shouted my mother from the front yard. I closed my eyes and stifled a groan, ashamed of my mother once again.

Dean gently placed my feet on the ground as he stood up, ready to face my mother once again. As we reached the door, Dean took a quick peek outside, and there she was in her car, ranting and raving. The funniest part was even in my mom's furious state, she didn't have enough courage to come up to Dean's parent's front door.

Some of Constantine's neighbors started to wander outside to see what the commotion was all about.

"If you don't send my daughter out right now, I will kill everyone in your house!" Helga shouted.

At that moment, half of the spectators pulled out their cell phones, no doubt to call the police because there might be a possible threat.

"Stay inside, Hailey. I don't want you anywhere near her when she is like that," Dean said, and before I could refuse, he kissed me on the top of my head, and Dean and his dad, Charlie, walked out toward my mother.

I didn't go inside, but I didn't go toward my mom either. Instead, I stayed on the front porch of the house because I wanted to hear everything that was said.

"What do you want, Helga?" Dean asked, sounding more polite than he should.

"I want my daughter!" she hissed in response.

"Well, you kicked her out, remember?" Dean pointed out.

"I gave her an option to leave. But I don't think I like her choice!" Helga shouted.

"Well, that's not for you to decide anymore. She doesn't want to go back home. Now I'm going to ask you to please go home, and if Hailey wants you in her life, she will contact you. All I want is Hailey's happiness," Dean bargained.

"No, you'll send her out right now. If you don't, I will call the police. Don't forget, Dean, you are older than my daughter. She is underage and you're not, even if it is a two-year difference. I will call the police and tell them you kidnapped her," my mother bragged.

"Go ahead, I'm not afraid of your threats, Mrs. Wyatt." And with that sentence Dean started to walk away. "Oh, by the way"—Dean turned around to face my mother one more time—"I would be happy to go to jail for her. She's worth it." He walked toward me and grasped my hand and looked into my eyes to see what I wanted to do. So I followed my heart. I gripped his hand back and pulled him inside the house, closing the door behind us.

"Did you hear what was said out there?" Dean asked, turning his attention to his mom.

"I think the whole neighborhood heard. For the record, I'm not okay with you going to jail," she chided. "I do have a plan though. Were you two serious about getting married?"

"Yes," we both answered at the same time and chuckled.

"Okay, well then, congratulations. You guys now have a wedding date: today," she announced.

"How is that even possible?" Dean asked.

"Don't worry, I'll take care of it." Constantine answered.

She was faithful to her word; she definitely took care of it. She called a local pastor, who did marriages anywhere as long as you had a marriage license, and he only did the ceremonies during certain hours. She even paid two hundred dollars for him to come out. She set up a ceremony area in the living room and called all of Dean's brothers and sister while I called Simone. Thirty minutes later, I was in a dress. Just like everything else in my life, my wedding wasn't what you would consider a typical wedding. It was different and unique, just the way I would want it to be. My dress went just barely past my knees, and it was a dark purple. Constantine zipped the zipper up my back as I ran my fingers over the material of the dress. The dress wasn't silk, and a well-known designer didn't make it. However, the dress was perfect for me. I liked simple, I liked odd, everything that this dress was. It certainly made a statement. The dress had patterns on it as well as flowers but not roses or lilies but Hawaiian flowers. Strange for a wedding dress, but I didn't care what I got married in. All I cared about was who I was going to marry.

"Here, put these on," Constantine said, handing me a pair of black dress flats.

"Thank you." I smiled back at her.

"Okay, so let's see, wedding checklist," Constantine counted out. "A dress, check. Something borrowed—that would be the shoes—so check. Now something old." She paused and walked over to her dresser and quickly flipped open one of her jewelry boxes. "Yes, this will do," she commented as she pulled out a silver bracelet, and by looking at it, I could tell it was old. The silver showed signs of wear, and I couldn't help but to run my fingers over the cold silver as Constantine clasp the bracelet around my wrist.

"This was my mother's. Take care of it, and please make sure I get this back, okay?" she asked and continued before I could answer. "Never mind, I know I can trust you."

"Now for something blue. Stay right here. I have the perfect thing." She dashed out of the room. When she came back into the room, she was holding a bouquet of blue daisies.

"Where did you get these?" I questioned as she handed me the flowers.

"They're fake." She laughed. "And I had them lying around."

"I think you are in the wrong line of business. You have put a wedding together in almost an hour. Thank you for doing this, for everything. This is more than I could ever hope for, seeing as we had such a fast deadline," I whispered.

"You make Dean happy, and that's what I want most for him," she reassured, and tears started to spring to my eyes because that's all I wanted, but my worst fear was that I couldn't give it to him.

"Hey, none of that. Everything will be fine, and here, I found something new for you." She opened her hand and revealed a necklace. "This is my wedding gift to you." The pendant's design was of an angel.

"Thank you. This means so much to me," I said as I turned around so that Constantine could clasp the necklace around my neck.

"There. We have everything we need. Are you ready?"

"Yes, I am."

I entered the ceremony area and saw that the pastor had arrived already, and he was talking to Dean. Dean turned around, and I had to stop my mouth from hitting the floor; he looked so handsome. Dean had an all-black attire from his shirt down to his shoes, but he looked incredibly hot. He seemed so at ease and happy while he stood there with the pastor. Even though he was wearing all black, his bright smile screamed, "I am getting married!"

I took a deep breath as I walked toward Dean and the pastor. As I reached them, again it felt like something in me settled when Dean gave me his boyish smile. I felt something tug in my chest as I felt like another piece of my torn heart was mended a little.

"Are we ready to proceed?" the pastor asked both Dean and me as Constantine lined everyone up. On Dean's side stood his brothers, Donovan and Kyle. On my side stood my friend Simone and Dean's sister Mable. What a sight everyone made. Only Dean and I were in formal type clothes, and everyone else but Kyle was in jeans and a T-shirt. Kyle had rushed over from his job and was currently covered head to toe in grease. Yet I still didn't care; this was my new family, and they were as odd and kind as I was.

"Yes," we said together, finally answering the pastor, as Dean reached for my hand so he could intertwine our fingers together.

"Dear friends and family, we are gathered here today to witness and celebrate the union of Dean Heart and Hailey Wyatt," the pastor begun.

"Upon arriving here, I had the pleasure of speaking to the young man in front of me. I wanted to try and gain an understanding of the couple I will be joining today, and I must say I learned quite a bit," the pastor stated.

"In the short time they have known each other, their love and understanding of each other has grown and matured, and now they have decided to live their lives together as husband and wife," the pastor proceeded. Do you, Dean, take Hailey to be your wife, to have and to hold from this day forward, for better or for worse, for richer and poorer, in sickness and in health, to love and to cherish from this day forward until death do you part?"

Within a second, Dean replied, "I do."

And my heart skipped a beat. He just agreed to spend the rest of his life with me. There was no hesitation. Just complete sincerity and dedication.

"Do you, Hailey, take Dean to be your husband to have and to hold from this day forward, for better or for worse, for richer and for poorer, in sickness and in health, to love and to cherish from this day forward until death do you part?" With every word that he said, my heart seemed to speed up faster. I knew my answer already, and I knew I wouldn't ever second-guess it. "I do," I answered and was rewarded with a huge smile from Dean.

A blush crossed my skin as the pastor continued, "Now it is time for the exchanging of the rings, if you would, Dean," the pastor addressed.

"I, Dean, give you, Hailey, this ring as an eternal symbol of my love and commitment to you," Dean recited. As he slipped the ring on my finger, I looked at the ring and was amazed at what I saw. The ring was a gold band with an intertwined design of the infinity symbol, and where the band crossed, there were two names engraved there. One side read *Dean* with his birthstone and on the other side was my name and my birthstone. I looked up into Dean's eyes and let him see my complete shock.

"I bought it the day you told me yes… the first time I asked you," Dean informed me as if he knew exactly what I was thinking.

My heart melted, and I struggled to keep my tears at bay.

"This one here is mine," he said as he produced a silver band, and I took a quick glance at it, seeing that the band was a typical silver band except for the engraving on the front of it. Dean had engraved the claddagh symbol on his ring.

"I, Hailey, give you, Dean, this ring as an eternal symbol of my love and commitment to you," I recited as I slid the ring into his finger.

"And now, by the power vested in me by the state of Arizona, I now pronounce you husband and wife," the pastor announced. "You may now kiss the bride."

Dean gently grabbed me, and before he kissed me, he whispered in my ear, "Finally, I can really call you mine." Then he kissed me so passionately that I didn't realize that I had wrapped my arms around his neck, pulling him closer to deepen our kiss. As the happiness swept through me, the pastor cleared his throat, informing us that our kiss was turning into a not-so-wedding-like kiss.

"Family and friends, I present to you Mr. and Mrs. Heart," the pastor announced after we broke from our kiss, and the small group erupted into applause. "Now if you will please follow me, I would like us to head to the dining area so we can do the certificate signing," the pastor instructed.

Everyone started to follow the pastor, and Dean tugged me in tow with hands still intertwined. As we approached the table in the dining area, I saw a marriage certificate sitting there, and from the looks of it, it had already been filled out. The only thing that was needed to make the document official was signatures. "Friends and family, to conclude this ceremony, will the designated witnesses please come forward and sign their names to the certificate of marriage?" the pastor asked.

Mable stepped forward and signed her name stating to the pastor that she was my witness.

"Freeze and pose for a picture, Mable," Constantine asked nicely, so Mable did just as she was asked. Then Donovan went and proceeded to do the same thing.

"Now if Mr. and Mrs. Heart will please come forward and sign your names on the marriage certificate."

Dean and I stepped forward one at a time; I went first, and I stopped and posed so Constantine could take some more pictures after we signed.

"Well, everything is now official. Unless you need anything else from me, I should get going now," the pastor announced, informing our little group that the wedding had officially concluded.

"Thank you for coming as soon as you did, and thank you for doing the service for us." Dean replied as he shook the pastor's hand.

I stayed in the kitchen, staring at the marriage license as Dean walked the pastor to his car. I waited for some kind of shock to settle in because now at the age of seventeen, I had gotten married, yet all I felt was happiness, complete and total satisfaction.

"Hello, Mrs. Heart," Dean said as he came up behind me, encasing me in an embrace.

"Hello, Mr. Heart," I replied, a smile spreading across my face.

"Any regrets yet?" Dean asked, and I quickly turned around to face him only to see concern on his face.

"No, why would you think that?" I asked, trying to soothe him.

"I don't know, sweetheart, but I do want you to know that when you turn eighteen, if you don't want this or us anymore, just let me know. I would never hold it against you. All I want is for you to be happy even if it's without me," Dean blubbered, holding his breath awaiting my response.

"Dean, when I said my vows, I meant every word. I didn't say them just to take them back in a year. When I said them, I meant them forever, so now you're stuck with me," I teased, and I quickly placed a kiss on his lips, hoping to calm his worries, but before I pulled away, Dean's hands crept around me, preventing me from stepping away. He deepened our kiss, and just like every other time, I lost myself in it. Dean was the first one to pull away, and I knew it was in order to look down at his watch.

"As much as I would love to stay, I have to go to work," Dean breathed.

"Really, even today, it is our wedding day and all," I begged.

"I'll be back late tonight, sweetheart, but I have to go to work. I have a wife to support now," he said and pulled my hand to his mouth, kissing my wedding band. "I think I'm going to enjoy that word a lot, *wife*. I love you, wife. My wife." And he kissed me one more time before grabbing his car keys and heading out the door.

CHAPTER 8

My New Family

*The bond that links your true family is not one of
blood, but of respect and joy in each other's life.*
—*Richard Bach*

The bright light came pouring through the small cracks of the blinds as I slowly became more awake. I covered my hands over my face, and I felt the cold metal of my ring and quickly glanced at it. Relief swept through me because a part of me was afraid that I might have dreamt the whole thing: meeting Dean, falling in love, getting married, but as I glanced at the gold band, I realized that it was all real, and this was my life now.

"Ahhhh, it's too bright," Dean groaned next to me.

"Then you get up. I'm too tired," I giggled as I rolled over and wrapped my body around his.

"What time did you get home last night?" I asked, a little sad to have spent our wedding night alone.

"I came home around three. I had to stay behind to lock up," he replied as he wrapped his arms around me. "What's on the agenda for today?" he asked, trying to snuggle closer.

"Well, I have school, and I start work today." I sighed, realizing that reality would always come to pop my little bliss bubble.

As we pulled up in front of my high school, I went over with Dean what I had to do in order to change the information with school.

"Don't worry, I know what I need to do. I'll take care of it," I reassured Dean and then kissed him good-bye as I raced out of the car in order to make it to my first period.

I made it into the class just as the bell rang and walked straight up to my history teacher, Mr. Jenkins. "Can I have a moment with you, Mr. Jenkins?" I asked, keeping my voice as low as possible.

"Sure, Hailey. Is everything okay at home?" Mr. Jenkins asked as we stepped outside the classroom. Mr. Jenkins was one of the very few adults who knew how my home life was. He was a teacher I've known for about three years now. He also had my older sister in his class four years ago, so he was also, unfortunately, around to see a few of my mother's episodes.

"I'm a lot better now. I need some advice. Dean and I got married yesterday, and I wanted to know how to go about informing the school of this?" I asked.

"Wow! Congrats, you two, and I only ask this next question as a concerned adult, are you pregnant? Do you guys need help?" Mr. Jenkins asked, and I could tell he was sincerely concerned.

"No, it's nothing like that. Helga went nuclear, and so we pushed up the wedding date." I laughed.

"Okay, well, I saw that coming sadly, and we'll have my teacher aide handle the class, and I'll go with you to the office and speak on your behalf," Mr. Jenkins informed me before walking back into class to talk to his assistant.

Not much was said as we walked to the office, and once we were at the front desk, Mr. Jenkins took care of everything.

"Yes, hello, can you please let Hailey Wyatt's counselor know that we need to have a meeting with her ASAP?" Mr. Jenkins announced to the receptionist. She slipped into the back area of the office where the counselors' offices were located. A few moments later, she came back with Mrs. Silverman in tow.

"What can I do for you, Mr. Jenkins?" she asked rudely, and I can only imagine we must have been interrupting something.

"I was hoping we could speak in private," Mr. Jenkins stated politely.

"Yes, of course. Please follow me this way," she replied.

When we got to her office, Mr. Jenkins went over the events that I told him, and I filled in the rest of the blanks for Mrs. Silverman.

"Well, that is definitely a problem now, isn't it?" Mrs. Silverman concluded after our conversation.

"Yes, that's why I thought it best to inform you, her guidance counselor, on what was going on," Mr. Jenkins stated.

"Yes, that was very smart of you. Well, I need to go collect a few things for Hailey, and I'll be right back," Mrs. Silverman announced before she walked out of the room.

"What could she possibly be getting?" Mr. Jenkins asked, sounding a little confused with how fast Mrs. Silverman left.

"You know counselors. She is going to come back with a bunch of self-help packets," I replied, trying to stifle a giggle. Mr. Jenkins, on the other hand, just started to laugh nonstop.

"Oh my god, that was awesome, Hailey."

A few minutes later, Mrs. Silverman wanders back into the room with papers in hand. "Sorry. Had a phone call to make, but here are some documents you need to fill out now that you are married. Also here are some packets on what to expect and also some programs that might help you," Mrs. Silverman explained. Before she could continue, Mr. Jenkins started to chuckle. "Is something wrong, Mr. Jenkins?" Mrs. Silverman asked, offended by Mr. Jenkins's behavior.

"No, sorry, had a little tickle in my throat. Please continue," Mr. Jenkins replied, and I could see he was trying hard not to laugh again. My guess was because I was completely right about the pamphlets.

"Mr. Jenkins, if you don't mind, I'd like Hailey to miss her first-period class so I may answer any questions she might have," Mrs. Silverman requested.

"That's fine, but if it's okay with Hailey, I'd like to stay and help to answer and ask some questions as well," Mr. Jenkins stated.

"I don't think that is entirely appropriate, Mr. Jenkins," Mrs. Silverman suggested.

"Yes, this may be true, but the decision isn't up to us now, is it? Hailey is an adult now, so how about we let her decide?" Mr. Jenkins voiced. *Finally, I get to speak*, I thought before I voiced my reply.

"Well, I would prefer Mr. Jenkins to stay. He has been one of the few adults that I have come to trust entirely." Before Mrs. Silverman could object, I continued with my thoughts. "Also, I do appreciate you taking time to answer my questions, but I don't have any. Thanks to my husband, I have a full-time supportive family. I also have loyal friends and fantastic teachers. I couldn't ask for anything more, but if I do ever have any questions, I will definitely make an appointment with you, Mrs. Silverman."

There was a sudden hesitation with her reply. "Well, let me just make sure you have everything," she muttered. She proceeded for the next twenty minutes finding more reasons for me to stay. It hit me then what she was trying to do: she was attempting to stall, but why? At that exact moment, I glanced out the office window and saw the reason.

What I saw suddenly sent fear skittering through my blood stream. My mother was there at my high school and heading straight for the office. I didn't know what to do, and at that moment, I felt like a cat trapped in a corner. I stumbled out of my seat, knocking it over and causing it to make a loud thud. I pushed myself up against the nearest wall, hoping that it would calm me down. At least she couldn't come up to me from behind.

"Hailey, what's wrong?" Mr. Jenkins asked; concern was strong in his voice.

"She called her. I don't want to go back. Don't let her take me back," I said, mumbling before I slid to the floor putting my head into my folded arms.

"What is she talking about?" Mr. Jenkins asked as he turned from me to face Mrs. Silverman.

"I called her mother. As her guidance counselor, I thought it would be in Hailey's best interest if she and her mother talked about this and worked it out," she replied her tone a little cold. "She is just too young to get married. She is only a child, and she is going to ruin her life. She can't possibly know what love is, and she can't possibly know what is right for herself."

"That was not a decision for you to make, and you have no idea what that woman has put this girl through. Just look at her!" Mr. Jenkins yelled. I glanced up and met Mrs. Silverman's eyes so she could see every emotion, all the pain, and every heartbreak.

"Well then, I'll go speak with her," Mrs. Silverman blurted out and soon averted her eyes from my gaze.

"No, I think you've done enough already, Mrs. Silverman. I'll take care of this," Mr. Jenkins replied before he stormed from the office. I don't know what was discussed, but five minutes later, when Mr. Jenkins returned to the room, my mom was gone and had been escorted off the premises as he had put it.

When Dean and I returned to his parents' house later that day, I was already exhausted. After this morning's events, I called Dean and told him about what happened and that the school was informed that my mother was no longer allowed on campus and that I wanted to finish up the school day.

Unfortunately for me, I was not expecting there to be guests at the house when we got there. It turned out that while I was at school and Dean was at work, Constantine made some calls to their entire family announcing the new marriage.

"Everyone, they're here," Constantine announced throughout the house.

"Who's everyone?" I asked, my nerves starting to set in.

"Oh, don't worry, it's only half of the family." Constantine chuckled. "Come on, there's no need to be shy. You are now part of the family after all," she continued.

Dean and I followed her to the living room where a large group of people was waiting. One by one, we were greeted and congratulated. Donovan and his girlfriend went first, and just like all of Dean's family, Donovan was very kind although he never seemed to date any woman who was very kind. Kyle and Simone went next, and I calmed at their presence because I knew that I had at least two people who were happy about our marriage. Next was Charlie, Dean's dad, who gathered me in a big hug and said, "I am very pleased to have you as a daughter-in-law."

Dean gripped my hand and squeezed, and I knew he could see the tears gathering in my eyes. Mable came up and hugged her brother and congratulated both of us. I knew that Mable was sincere with her comment even though she didn't hug me; Mable was just that way, loving and kind, but it took her a while to warm up to people. Last to approach us was Julian, another one of Dean's brothers. I couldn't tell how he felt, and I never had been able to; that man had one hell of a poker face. After everyone was done, Constantine did what she always does and cooked dinner for everyone.

By the end of the night, everyone had left very full, and I had received three text messages: one was from Dean's sister Alice who was the only sibling not at the gathering, which wasn't even her fault because she lived out of town. "Welcome to the family. Mom gave me your number. I know we haven't met yet, but I know you're right for my brother because I can hear the love in his voice. Take care of him."

The second was from one of my closest friends Molly: "You bitch. Thanks for telling me that you got married. I had to hear it through the gossip mill, which by the way, your marriage is spreading around school like wildfire. Even though I wasn't invited to the event, I am happy for both Dean and you." That was Molly, sweet but fierce, and I sent her back a quick reply with the reason why the wedding was low-key.

The third and final message was from my other close friend Lana: "Wow, marriage. That's a big step... Well, congrats." To others, that message might seem cold, but I knew Lana, and it wasn't that commitment scared her; it just worried her.

I headed toward our room, and once in the safety of the walls, I collapsed onto the bed. I ran my hands over the padded comforter, and I couldn't help but to cry after everything that had happened. I finally had the family I always wanted, and I was given the love and support that I never received from my mother. Even though I was extremely happy, there was a part of me that was sad.

"Hey, baby, what's wrong?" Dean comforted as he pulled me into his arms. I must have been crying hard because I hadn't even realized he had come into the room.

"Nothing, I'm just really happy," I replied, knowing that my breakdown was now over.

"You don't sound fine, and I may be new at this husband thing, but I think crying is not a good thing," Dean replied, slightly amused.

"No! I am happy. You've given me so much, Dean. I mean it. I just think I had to let out all the sadness I've been carrying with me for all these years in order to be able to let my heart open up all the way and to be able to heal more." And then I kissed him, putting everything into that kiss.

"Okay, I believe you. You're okay," Dean stated, his breathing now heavy.

"Dean, can I ask you for something?" I whispered as my cheeks started to turn red.

"Of course, baby, you can ask anything of me, and I will do everything I can to make it happen," Dean responded.

"Make me truly yours," I whispered in his ear because it seemed like it was what I wanted at that moment more than anything else in the world. It was the only thing I could think to say. I have never done anything sexual before. Dean was my first everything, and he was going to be my last everything.

"What?" Dean asked, and I felt a shudder go through his body.

"Please, I need something right now that I know no one can ever take from me," I begged.

"Are you sure?" Dean asked, afraid of me maybe regretting my choice later.

"Yes," I coaxed as I took his lips again and gave into the burning need that I have been feeling ever since the first time he looked at me.

Afterward, I hid in our bed and snuggled under the covers, trying to hide the giant grin on my face.

"I'll be right back. I'm going to go clean up," Dean said before he kissed me and darted out of the room.

A few minutes later Dean came staggering back into the room, and I became instantly alarmed when I saw that his face was now three shades whiter.

"Dean, what's wrong?" I asked, quickly jumping out of bed, wrapping the blanket around my body as I approached him.

"We might have a slight problem. I think the condom broke." Dean cursed.

CHAPTER 9

Surprise!

The moments of happiness we enjoy take us by surprise.
It is not that we seize them, but that they seize us.
—Ashley Montagu

It had been nearly two weeks since Dean's confession that we might be parents. Even though that was a small amount of time, it seemed to have dragged on forever. We still had at least three more weeks until we could take a test to know if I was carrying Dean's child or not. School was finishing up in less than a month, and I still had a whole year of high school left before I graduated, and now a baby possible due in nine months. The worst part is I could see how much Dean was struggling with this, and even though he wouldn't say so, I knew he blamed himself. I know that he didn't regret the baby, if there was one. I knew he blamed himself for possibly making me pregnant before I was ready. I grew up in a home where I couldn't do what I wanted to do and what made me happy. With a baby, I would be happy, but going to college or having a night life wouldn't really be an option.

I walked down the hallway in a trance, thinking about everything that has happened in the past two weeks—from Dean looking for more work to looking at what a baby needs, to looking into my school options, to me panicking that maybe Dean didn't want kids and because I always have wanted kids, he would do the right thing and stay with me and his child but be miserable for the rest of his life. Suddenly my phone buzzed, snapping me out of my trance. I quickly glanced at the text so I could reply before my next class period started.

"I just wanted you to know that I love you, and if you are pregnant, I'm going to do everything I can to be a great father." I placed my hand over my stomach, and I don't know how, but deep down in my heart, I knew that I was pregnant. I knew that Dean and I were going to be all right because we were going to love this baby with all our hearts, and just like everything in our lives that we had had to face, we were going to face this together.

Sure enough, we soon confirmed that I was indeed pregnant, and even though we were young, scared, and had no idea what we were doing, Dean and I couldn't help but to be happy. One accident turned into a beautiful miracle, and after a while, Dean and I became less scared about the fact that we would soon be parents of an innocent baby. We started to plan everything out. Dean and I would get jobs in order to save up for when the baby arrived. As for school, when it started back up, I would be going to a work at your own pace high school. How they work is they allow you to be in control of the credits you need to earn. You can complete the work whenever and as fast as you want. That way if I was able to work hard enough and get the rest of the credits I needed to graduate fast enough, I could graduate early. The part that did scare us was telling Dean's mom because if she didn't support this little human being coming into this world, we would be truly on our own.

I was beginning to realized that Dean's mother tried to get the family together every chance she could, because when I got home she was making dinner for the whole family. I walk through the door and was greeted by a kitchen full of people. I don't know why I was surprised Dean's family always had these huge parties for holidays and birthdays, so considering the size of his family there were parties all the time. Even with all the celebrations, sometimes Dean's family just liked to get together for dinners. It was one of those days, so we figured that it would be a good time to tell everyone the news, but first we needed to tell Constantine.

"Hey, Mom, can we talk with you outside for a moment?" Dean whispered to his mom.

She glanced at me, then replied, "That sentence is beginning to worry me because it always means something is going on." But she followed us outside anyways.

Dean started to speak once he closed the doors leading to the patio, but he didn't get too far into his sentence, "Mom, we have something to tell you, and please—"

"Hailey's pregnant right?" Constantine asked.

"How did you know?" I asked stunned at the fact that she was already aware of the news.

"Baby girl, nothing happens underneath this roof that I'm not aware of," Constantine commented.

"That still doesn't explain how you knew," I stated completely amazed.

"It's a little hard to explain, but I just know things," Constantine continued when she saw my mouth drop open. "If you think that's freaky, I can guess the sex of the baby, and I'm always correct." I looked toward Dean, and he knew exactly what I was thinking.

"She's telling the truth," he informed me.

"Well, congratulations, and my guess is that you're having a girl," Constantine added. Before we could say anything back, Constantine opened the doors to the house and called inside. "Hey everyone, come congratulate Dean and Hailey. They are going to be having a baby."

One by one, his family gave us their blessings, and I couldn't help but laugh when I heard how much of a hard time Dean's brothers were giving him.

"Didn't take you long to knock her up, did it? I think you might have beaten a world record," teased Kyle.

"Well, we Hearts do have champion swimmers." Donovan laughed.

"Don't lie, Dean. We all know it was your way of marking your territory," blurted Charlie.

"God, Dad, don't be gross," Dean countered.

"Well, unlike the rest of these idiots, I'm going to do what Mom said and say congrats, bro!" Julian shouted, and all the brothers chuckled in all together.

Dean looked over at me and smiled that boyish smile I love so much, and I know he was thinking the same thing I was; we weren't going to be without a family; instead this was just the beginning of one.

Three months went by in a flash as Dean and I were always on the go now that I was three months pregnant and was able to get good health insurance. We made our first appointment with an ob-gyn. The moment the doctor told us we had a healthy baby, we decided it was time to tell our closest friends because we didn't want to say anything until we felt it was time. Well, it didn't take long for the news to spread like wildfire at our old school. The worst part was we never knew that sharing the news would turn into one of the biggest trials of our lives. This was when we learned who we could actually call a friend. By the time the new school year had started and my high school friends found out that I was going to a new high school and I was starting a family, the calls and messages I used to receive came fewer and fewer until only a handful of friends remained. Even though I thought I would feel some sadness about the actual nature of those who I called friends for many years, the reality was that I was grateful to know who was really there for me.

Dean and I might now have had fewer friends, but we at least still had some of our closest friends. Dean's childhood friend of twelve years, Fredrick, who had always been by Dean's side, immediately congratulated us and had been constantly asking if there was anything we need. Fredrick was the only constant friend Dean had ever had his entire life, so when he turned out to be the only one there for Dean, we weren't surprised at all nor was Dean upset. I, on the other hand, still had the girls, Simone, Molly, Lana, and also Sam.

I had a feeling these friends would be the ones to stand by us because of how we met and how strong our bonds were. Dean met Fredrick when they were only ten years old. Fredrick had come over to Dean's house one day with one of Dean's other friend. He showed up, and that was it; they had been friends ever since. Dean had always been simple, so his friendship was the same way.

However, how I met my friends was anything but simple. I met Lana and Sam in class. It was in my freshman year, and because my family and I had moved yet again to another zip code, I had no friends. Lana and I met in math class and ended up bonding over our love in music. She was the one who told me about the school's soccer team, where I met Molly. I met Sam one day in Spanish class when I was being picked on by two girls twice my size. She inserted herself in between me and the girls, telling them that if they messed with me, they messed with her. How I met Simone still makes me laugh to this day. She had been friends with Lana first, and one day at lunch,, Lana invited me to join her. Once we reached the area where Lana said was her lunch spot, there was Simone standing on the lunch table shouting. She was dressed like a rock star with short blonde hair and was sporting a pair of steel-toe boots. She was upset because some guy kept trying to touch her, and I stood there and watched as the same guy reached for her again. Even though Simone is a very kind and happy person, we have learned over the years to not piss her off. Simone turned around and kicked the guy, landing a blow to his arm... breaking it. Not what she intended to do, but no one ever messed with her again.

In addition to being four months pregnant, I was starting my senior year at a new school. When I met Dean, he taught me not to care about the opinions of others. Now the only opinions that matter to me were from those who I held dear. I was in no way expecting the tidal wave of drama to rise at this new school.

"Please go ahead and take a seat in any available spot. We will begin with the rules and procedures for this school," the teacher said as she greeted me. I took the first empty seat I saw and waited for the class to begin. Soon after, a tall woman with brown hair and a slender build came in and addressed the class.

"Hello and welcome to Crest Mount High School. Today you are making the first step to taking your future into your own hands because here you can graduate as soon as you would like as long as you work hard. You can determine how long you stay here. If you work hard and receive enough credits, you can graduate any time you like," she announced to all sixty of us. "Now, all your class work and class studies are located on the campus computers that are at your desk, and each of you will have a student ID and password, that way only you can access your schoolwork," she continued. "Now just like any other high school, we have all the subjects here, but unlike other schools, we only have a few teachers to teach each subject. Don't be alarmed, our teachers here will have plenty of time to help each of you if you need any help with your studies. My name is Mrs. Barton, I am the principle here at Crest Mount, and if you have any issues, any concerns, or if you just want to talk, my door is open to you always," she boasted. "Now have a great school year." She then left us so we could begin our studies.

Another teacher stood up to address the class. "There are some papers on how to get started located at your desk. Also, if you want, please introduce yourselves to the people sitting next to you, but please keep the talking down to a minimum." I had two people sitting next to me, so I introduced myself to be friendly. Sitting to my right was a tall blond girl who had to have been the same age as me. She was dressed fashionably and had an air around her. I assumed it was due to her getting whatever she wanted all her life.

"Hello, my name is Hailey," I said introducing myself. I was at least expecting a response, but instead, she stared at me with a look on her face that screamed she thought I was crazy. Her gaze left my face and instantly jumped to my very now visible baby bump. Still, without having said a word, she smirked at me and pulled out a cell phone and started to type away. A few moments later, some of the girls behind her began to hackle away. Great, of all the places to sit, I had to sit next to the judging panel.

"Ignore them. Their opinion is only as valid as their IQs are, and seeing as they have an IQ of five, their opinion is invalid," whispered the guy sitting to my left. "My name is Seth, and if we want to survive, we girlfriends need to stick together," Seth stated in a feminine tone.

I smiled and spoke before I could stop myself, "Are you gay or just pretending so you can test me?"

"What? Why would you ask such an odd question?" Seth replied.

"No reason," I laughed. "Just something that happened to me once."

"So what do you say? Do you want to watch each other's assists?" Seth asked.

"Well, how 'bout I watch your back, but you watch my stomach. That needs more protection," I joked wanting to get the fact that I was pregnant out into the air.

"Good point. These bitches are bloodthirsty, not even unborn children are safe," he joked and then glared at the girls who were whispering, pointing, and giggling at us.

Two weeks into the school year, and the rumors just kept getting worse. There were rumors like I was carrying a secret love child that belonged to a married man and I used to sell my body for crack. These rumors were not very original, in the least, and to me they didn't even make any logical sense. I ignored all of them and just focused on my goal, and that was to graduate before the baby was born.

One day, Mrs. Barton called me into her office for a discussion. "Thank you for taking the time to speak with me, Hailey," she addressed me. "I've called you in here today so we might discuss a few things that have been brought to my attention."

"Mrs. Barton, let me stop you there. I know why you brought me in here. You brought me in here to talk about all the rumors that are going around about me, aren't you?"

"Yes, you could say that. We have had a few students come to us and tell us about your situation," she explained, and I figured out what she meant when I saw she was looking at my stomach. My hand instantly went to my stomach as a need arose in me to protect my child.

"Yes, I'm pregnant. It's not like I have polio," I fumed.

"Yes, I'm aware, but you didn't directly inform us of this when you decided to join our school," Mrs. Barton accused.

"I'm sorry, but there was no checkbox on the application that said 'Check this if you're pregnant.' I got in here based on my test scores. Also, I don't know how my condition hinders my learning in any way," I stated now upset.

"I agree, but your state seems to upset a few of our students, and they say you've been very unfriendly," she defended.

"Well, I didn't come here to make friends. I came here to get my education. I'm not the one spreading rumors, but that doesn't matter. When you accepted me into this school, you vetoed the right to deny me an education nor can you kick me out because I'm having a baby," I cursed. "So I'll make this easy for you. I'll earn my credits from home, that way I get what I want and your precious little students get to stay in their perfect little bubble. They won't have to deal with life, and no one here will have to see me until the graduation!" I shouted.

"Well, you could have put it a little nicer, but I'll have to agree with you!" Mrs. Barton exclaimed.

"Then I'll go collect my things and the rest of the work I need, and don't worry, I'll turn in my work, graduate, and then you'll never see me again," I continued as I opened the door.

"Wait, how will you be getting home?" Mrs. Barton asked, and I couldn't help but to laugh at the fact that now she was acting like a concerned adult.

"I'll have my husband pick me up," I answered, even though I didn't owe her an explanation.

"Oh, you're married," she said, sounding shocked.

"Yes, I am, and maybe if you had taken the time to find out, you would have discovered that I have a future, a plan for my life, and that I wasn't some stupid teenage girl." And with that last sentence, I walked out.

After I had collected my belongings, I went to find Seth. "Hey, sorry, but you might have to watch your own back from here on out," I informed.

"Hey, no worries. I heard what was said. The whole school heard, so I understand," Seth remarked.

"Wait, how could you hear?" I asked.

"Um, please, child, the whole school and I heard because this is a tiny building with paper walls. Oh, and before I forget, great job sticking it to the boss woman." Seth laughed and then walked away after saying his good-byes.

In three weeks, I finished all my work, received my credits and was informed that I would be able to graduate and go to my graduation ceremony where I would receive my diploma.

Consequently, good things only last for so long, and one morning Dean and I experienced one of our first life-changing events.

CHAPTER 10

The Accident

My life has been a whole series of accidents,
some of them happy, some not.
—Randy Bachman

"Hey, sweetheart, wake up," Dean cooed trying to wake me softly up.

"I don't wanna!" I laughed but rolled over to face him anyways.

"So last night someone shot out three of the Jeep's windows with a BB gun," Dean explained.

"Crap! What are we going to do?" I asked, sitting now fully up in bed.

"Well, you have been in bed for so long that it's already noon, and I've been out of bed since eight. I've already bought replacement windows, so I came in here to see if you wanted to help," Dean stated.

"Yes, I would love to help, so thank you for asking, but you can't blame me for sleeping in for so long, this baby is draining everything out of me." I giggled and got up to get dressed.

Outside I got to see the extent of the damage caused by the neighborhood punks. The back window, the passenger back window, and the driver rear window were all shot out. "Okay, so what do you need me to do to help?" I asked excitably.

"You, my sweet pregnant wife, get to sit in the front seat and play DJ," Dean stated as he opened the door for me like a perfect gentleman.

"Well, I do have excellent taste in music," I teased.

Soon after Dean finished installing the first window, he showed me his handy work. "There, looks good as new," Dean stated as he wiped down the window. "Onto the next one!" He proceeded onto the passenger side window and removed the damaged glass. I turned away from Dean, so I could play another song from the iPod. I chose "Whereever You Will Go" by The Calling as the next song and then turned my attention back to Dean, who was standing on the passenger side with the rear passenger door open and to his back.

It happen so fast that I barely saw the car coming straight for us before it suddenly rammed into ours, and I screamed as I saw the car clip Dean, but my scream was cut off as my head flew into the front window and a sudden darkness clouded my vision.

There was an extreme ringing in my ears as I tried to get a sense of what was going on. I placed my hands over my ears, hoping to soften the loud piercing sound. I wanted to attempt to open my eyes so I could see if Dean was all right, but the pain in my head wouldn't allow it. Once the ringing died down a little, I realized my name was being called, "Hailey! Baby, are you okay? Answer me, baby, I'm worried here!" Dean shouted.

"Yes, are you okay? The car… it hit you," I replied in a full panic now that I remembered what had happened.

"I got lucky, the car rammed into the door behind me. The door bent forward and hit me, but I am okay, baby," Dean reassured. "Is the baby ok?" Dean asked, and he placed his hand over my belly.

"Yes, I think so." I smiled.

"Okay. Stay right there, I'll be right back," Dean said.

Before I could ask him where he was going, Dean picked up the broom by our car and started running down the street shouting. I saw the reason for Dean's chase; the car that had struck us was trying to leave the scene but not succeeding. I couldn't sit still any longer and decided to carefully make my way toward Dean. The car seemed to be stalling and sputtering, the large dent in the front of the car possibly the cause. Both Dean and the vehicle had gotten halfway down the street before the car finally pulled over to the side of the road.

The vehicle was a 1996 gray station wagon with wood side panels. By the time I reached Dean, the driver's side door of the car swung open and out staggered a woman in her fifties. She was about five feet four inches, with brown hair, and I could tell that there was something not right about her.

"Oh my god, I am so sorry. Did I hit you guys?" the woman stammered as Dean walked up to her and the vehicle.

"Yes, you did," Dean replied calmly. "Can I ask you how it is possible that you hit my car? We were on the shoulder, out of the street, parked in front of our house. To hit us, you'd have to be driving on the wrong side of the road." Dean asked, taking a step toward the woman in order to see if she was all right. The woman quickly took a step away, almost as if she was trying to avoid getting too close to Dean.

"Yes, I am sorry about that, but I was driving down the street, and the sun got in my eyes," the woman stammered again now in a panicked tone.

"The sun was in your eyes for that long? We live half way down the street. Why didn't you pull over or stop?" Dean asked.

I sat down on the curb, no longer trusting my legs to support me. I wanted to stand next to Dean so I could hear the conversation even better, but my whole body wouldn't stop shaking.

"Well, I didn't pull over because the sun got out of my eyes before I had the chance to, but after I could see again, I spotted a large pothole and swerved to miss it," the woman yammered on.

"Ma'am, our streets just got repaved at the very beginning of this month," Dean informed, and I know he wasn't trying to call her a liar. He was only attempting to see what had happened and what almost cost us our lives.

"Well, my son had screamed out and told me to watch out for one, so I swerved," the woman claimed. Without hesitating, Dean ran to the woman's car in order to check her car. I could see the panic on Dean's face because he saw the woman come out of the car but not the child.

"Where's your son? There's nothing in this car but a box of toys and a tire," Dean asked, and his voice turned from worried to confused, which made two of us.

"Oh, he isn't here," the woman stated.

"But you just said... " Dean started to reply but stopped because he knew that the conversation was going nowhere.

"Well, I heard his voice telling me to watch out," the woman tried to explain.

By this time, Dean's mom had come outside and informed us that the police were on the way. I turned my attention back to Dean and the woman. "Well, how about we just wait until the police get here, and they can sort this all out," I announced.

"Wait, what?" the woman yelled, and I could see the panic written all over her face. "I can't stay that long. I need to get to work."

"I'm sorry, but we need to wait until the police arrive," Dean enforced, trying to calm the woman back down. Dean took another step toward her, and she immediately began to back away again.

"You don't understand! If I'm late for work, I will lose my job. I have a son. I can't afford to lose my job!" the women screamed. I already knew what Dean was going to say before he even said it.

"Okay, well how about you write down all your information so the police or I can get a hold of you if need be. That way, you can go to work. Please include your insurance information," Dean explained.

"Thank you so much!" the woman exclaimed, and she immediately started to scribble down her information on a piece of paper. After she and Dean exchanged information, she went on her way.

"I hope that wasn't a mistake," Dean commented.

The police arrived soon after and took pictures of the scene. As soon as the police informed us they were finished, Dean decided to take me to the hospital. He wanted to make sure that the baby was okay.

As we were waiting for the test results, Dean and I received a call from the police. It turned out that the woman who hit us gave us all correct information but left out some major details. She did, in fact, have a son but hasn't had a job in two years. Her car insurance is no good, and she even has warrants out for arrest. Now her behavior made complete sense, and Dean was livid at the news that the woman did not have car insurance.

"Sir, would you like to pursue her in order to take her to court?" the officer asked.

"No, it's fine. She seems to be having enough problems all on her own," Dean replied and then hung up the phone.

"Why aren't we going to sue her?" I asked so I could understand what was behind Dean's reasoning.

"I'm not doing it to help her. I am doing it for her son. He shouldn't have to keep paying for the choices his mother makes. If I take from her, I'm taking from that little boy as well," Dean explained.

"What are we going to do about the car? The baby is due in four months," I asked, worried about getting a safe vehicle for our child.

"We will figure something out. We always do, and I was looking into getting a new car anyway because our family is growing, and I have a feeling it's just going to get bigger and bigger."

The doctor came back, giving me and the baby a clean bill of health. As long as our child was safe, nothing else really mattered.

A whole month had passed since the accident, and finally the day both Dean and I had been looking forward to for a long time came. It was the day that we got to find out what the sex of the baby was. The morning of that day seemed to drag on forever, and Dean was nervously pacing the waiting room as we waited for the nurse to call us back.

"If you keep that up, you're going to leave a track in the carpet." I smirked as I watched Dean get more worked up by the minute.

"Hailey Heart, we are ready for you," the nurse called, and my excitement grew. The nurse brought us to a beautiful examination room and instructed that I change into a gown. Before the nurse left the room, she turned around and asked, "Do you want to know the sex of the baby, or do you want to keep it a secret?"

"We want to know!" Dean and I answered at the same time.

"Okay, I'll let the doctor know." The nurse laughed and then left the room.

The physician came into our room and informed us that the sonogram room was ready, so we followed her down the long corridor that led to large private rooms. Dean reached out and grabbed my hand, squeezing it, and I knew what he was thinking, that this was it. The room we entered was enormous and had a table next to the machine. Located on the wall was a fifty-four-inch flat-screen TV.

"Okay, please lie down on the table and lift up your gown," the doctor instructed. Once my gown was up, the doctor started the steps needed to do an ultrasound. "This might be cold," she warned as she squirted blue gel on my stomach and when it came to contact with my skin I jumped a little because it was indeed cold. "Sorry," she apologized as she used a wand to spread the gel over my enormous belly. "Okay, in a few short minutes, you guys are going to see your baby," the doctor announced, and right as she finished her sentence, the TV on the wall came to life, showing the picture of a tiny baby. "Are you guys ready to know what you are having?" Dr. Grey asked as she looked over at us.

"Yes, please." we replied with the same grins spreading across our faces.

"Well, congratulations you two! You are having a healthy baby girl," said Dr. Grey. Dean grabbed my hand and kissed my knuckles.

"She is beautiful." I whispered, and I couldn't help but to pull Dean down to me so I could kiss him.

Dean broke away and smiled bashfully at the doctor. "Can you print out some pictures for us?" Dean asked Dr. Grey.

We received the first pictures of our baby girl and a clean bill of health. Everything was finally falling into place.

CHAPTER 11

A New Arrival

Life is a flame that is always burning itself out, but
catches fire again every time a child is born.
—George Bernard Shaw

Everything was ready for the arrival of our baby girl, and our doctor told us she was going to be due around January 7, just one day after my eighteenth birthday. That day was fast approaching. We still lived with Dean's parents for the time being, and Dean and I had just one room, so we made the most of it for her. Dean painted the room a pea green color, and most of the baby stuff we needed was given to us at our baby shower. I was so happy and amazed to see how many people showed up. We received a crib, bassinet, and a lot of clothes from Constantine. Dean's friends Stacy, Monica, and Joel all pitched in to buy us a stroller and car seat. Everyone else bought odds and ends: clothes, diapers, and bottles. The biggest gift we received was from my amazing aunt Cathy; she gave us the last thing we needed before the baby came. She gave us enough money for us to be able to put a down payment on a car. I would have never accepted such a generous gift if it weren't for the fact that we needed a car for when the baby arrived.

My aunt Cathy is my mother's sister, and even though they have the same blood running through their veins, they were in no way alike. Cathy has been there for me as long as I could remember. She is a kind, loving, and amazing women. She has been there for us, not only in our time of need but also just everyday stuff. The one thing that my aunt does that shows just how big of a heart she has is that even if her life is stressful, she still texts me every day and checks in on me. When I was growing up, I used to be very close with my aunt and loved to spend time with her, but nothing good in my life ever stayed around long, thanks to my mother. One day, out of the blue, Helga informed us her kids that we were no longer speaking to my aunt and that I, especially, was no longer allowed to visit her, not now, not ever. When I questioned my mother, I was informed that Cathy insulted my mom in some way. That's when it hit me; my aunt must have disagreed with my mom in some way, so my mom lied to us in order to try and stick it to my aunt. As soon as I married Dean, I contacted Cathy because my mom no longer had control over me, and I know that my aunt was just as happy as I was that we could have our relationship again. To me, my relationship with my aunt felt more like a mother-daughter relationship than an aunt and niece, and I preferred it that way. Cathy was more of a mother to me than Helga ever was; she never said hurtful things or judged me, and she loved me with her whole heart and never expected anything in return.

The car we ended up getting was a green 2001 Isuzu Trooper, and it was in almost new condition. We felt lucky to have found such a great car in a used car lot.

As the date grew closer, Dean became more and more restless. When he wasn't looking at baby information online, I would watch him drift and pace all over the house. He was starting to remind me of those caged tigers you see at the zoo. He wasn't the only one nervous about the big day coming up very soon; I was turning into a nervous wreck also. My nerves were more fear than anything else, and the dreams I was starting to have were only making things worse.

Lately, I was dreaming about my hidden fears in regard to my upcoming motherhood, and even though I tried to ignore it, I knew I had to come to terms with what my fears were. I was afraid that I would turn into the horrible monster of a parent my mother had been. She may have never beaten us, but the emotional abuse was far more painful than anything she could have ever done to us physically. I had to live with my scars on the inside, and no one could see them but me. I lived every day fighting my inner demons to prove to them and myself that I am not who my mother said I was. The thing that scared me the most was that my mom had not always been that way. My grandparents used to tell me that my mom was dedicated, fierce, and loving, yet as I look at her, I could no longer see any traces of the woman she once was. I never want to put my innocent child through what I went through; I was hoping that if I did turn into the woman who haunted my dreams as a child, I would stop myself before I ever hurt my child. Little did I know that when I gazed into the eyes of my baby girl, all my worries and doubts would go away forever.

The date was January 27, 2009, and I was two weeks overdue. The doctor suggested that it was time for the baby to come so instead of waiting for her to come on her own, the doctor sent me to the hospital so I could be induced. Waiting longer than two weeks past my due date could put the baby in potential danger, so Dean and I agreed to have the induced labor. Inducing labor is a method used to start stimulating the childbirth process in a woman. We went to the hospital around five to start the process. We didn't officially begin until I received the medication at seven o'clock, and then the count-down begun. Around midnight, I was still having trouble sleeping, and I needed all the sleep I could get, so my nurse gave me something to help me sleep, and boy was it strong. Before she let me take the pill, she called in my doctor and asked her if I should get my epidural before I went to bed. She explained to me that the medication was so strong that if I went into full-blown labor in my sleep, I wouldn't be able to get an epidural. I chose to get it before I went to sleep because I thought it was better to be safe than sorry. I didn't think I could handle a painful delivery, and a few minutes later, I was sitting up on my bed while an anesthesiologist stuck a longer needle into my spine. When she described what she would be doing to me, I got freaked out, but it wasn't as bad as I had thought it would be. There was a little poke, then nothing.

"All done," the doctor informed me, and I decided to take my tiny white pill so I could sleep.

I wanted to use the restroom before I couldn't work my legs anymore, and in the time it took to pee and come back out into the room, everything was spinning. Things started to turn into weird shapes and colors, and my legs began to feel heavier. As I entered the room, Dean jumped up, and I knew he could tell something was wrong.

"Are you okay?" Dean asked, and I smiled because his concern touched me.

"Yes, just tired, and everything looks weird," I replied, and Dean started to laugh. "You look orange, and your hands are enormous," I explained to him so he knew exactly what I was seeing.

Dean went and grabbed a computer chair that was in our room, and he shut off the lights. He then proceeded to grab both of our cell phones and turn on the flashlight app so he could pretend he was a space ship. Dean started to make weird noises and spin on the computer chair very fast. At first, his goofiness rubbed off on me, and I couldn't stop myself from giggling, and then the dizziness got much worse, and I almost toppled over. I was waiting to hit the floor when I realized Dean had caught me. He must've turned on the lights and saw me falling.

"I'm sorry, sweetheart. I didn't mean to hurt you. I was only playing," Dean said as he picked me up and carried me to bed.

"Shh, it's okay. It wasn't your fault. It's the medication," I comforted. "I'm just sleepy," I said as my eyes started to drift closed.

"Okay, go to bed, baby. I'll be next to you the entire time," Dean had whispered before darkness claimed me.

Dean was true to his word, and I was awakened in the morning by my nurse who had come in to check to see how far I dilated. I found Dean asleep. At some point during the night, Dean must have pulled the couch closer to my bed because now he was so close I could reach out and touch him. I felt sorry for Dean because he looked so uncomfortable on that tiny pull-out bed. I could tell from looking at it that it was hard and too small for Dean's big frame.

The nurse lifted the blanket that was covering my lower half, and I adjusted myself so she could check my progress.

"Holy cow!" the nurse exclaimed, and I couldn't tell if her comment meant something good or bad. She placed the sheet back over me and looked at me with a brilliant smile on her face. "Your daughter has beautiful hair," she informed me, and I was then in full-blown shock. How could she see her hair? The nurse went over and woke up my husband "Mr. Heart, sir, you need to wake up. Your daughter is going to be here soon."

And that's all it took. Dean shot right up and was in action mode.

"I am going to go get the doctor now," the nurse said and left the room.

Everything after that went by in a blur; the doctor came in, and everyone started setting everything up. I was moved to the delivery room and would return to my previous room once our daughter was born. Dean excused himself from the room for a moment in order to use the restroom; the room we were in now didn't have a restroom, so he had to go down the hall. Dean thought that we were going to be in labor for a while, so when he received a message over the intercom in the bathroom, he was surprised.

"Mr. Heart, if you don't hurry back to the room, you're going to miss the birth of your first child," the intercom shouted out. A moment later, Dean was in the room and holding my hand.

"Okay, whenever you're ready, start pushing," Dr. Grey stated, and I felt the nerves in my stomach grow bigger and bigger. I didn't know if I could do this. Could I actually give another human being everything they need? Could I be the mom this child needed? What happen if—

My thoughts were cut off by Dean squeezing my hand. I wasn't alone in this, and I knew together, we would help each other, so I pushed and pushed again.

"Okay, those were great. One more big push, and she should be here," Dr. Grey cheered.

So I pushed again, and I put everything I had into this one, and I didn't stop until I heard a loud cry. I opened my eyes and saw Dr. Grey holding a little white-and-red-covered baby.

"Congrats, it's a beautiful baby girl," Dr. Grey announced as the nurse handed her a blanket so she could swaddle the baby. The doctor rushed her to a bedding area so she could examine our baby girl. A second later, she was in my arms, and I felt something in my heart pull like another broken piece had fallen into place. As I looked down at our little girl, a tear escape and rolled down my cheek because I had never seen anything so amazing but defenseless. She was a part of me and a part of Dean; she was the good of us put into one amazing child. She was the result of our struggle and our love. I knew that my earlier fears were gone because I would protect this child with my life, and I would be the best mother I could be for her. They took her away so they could weigh, clean, and check her vitals once again.

"Have you chosen a name for her yet?" a nurse asked, and Dean answered for the both of us.

"Her name is Elizabeth Kay Heart," he said proudly, and he then leaned down to capture my lips with his. "Thank you for giving me her. You have made me the happiest man in the world, again." Dean straightened back up as the nurse came back around with a now clean Elizabeth. The nurse started to hand her back to me, but I shook my head and pointed at my husband, the new daddy who looked like he couldn't wait to hold his baby girl.

"She weighs seven pounds, nine ounces and is eleven inches long," Dr. Grey told us, and Dean held Elizabeth close to his chest, whispering to her that he was her daddy.

CHAPTER 12

Surprise Part 2

Surprise is the greatest gift which life can grant us.
—Boris Pasternak

Dean's family fell head over heels in love with Elizabeth, and it didn't take long for our friends to become smitten with her as well. After her birth, time went by fast as Dean and I picked up on parenthood quickly. Elizabeth made it easy to be parents, and she always kept us on the go; there were many sleepless nights and colds to fight. She made us melt with her sweetness and laugh with her silly personality. She made everything worth it. Helga found out that I had a baby, and she desperately tried to become part of our family again. She promised to get help, but I knew she never would, and no matter how much she begged, I never let her back in our lives because I knew if she couldn't be a mother for me, she never would be a good grandmother for my daughter. You cannot choose who to love and who not to love, and she shouldn't want to be a better person just because she wasn't allowed to see her grandchild. She should have wanted to be a better person so she could have her own child back in her life.

When Elizabeth was two months old, I received a call from my high school saying that a graduation date was set, and because I had earned all the credits I needed, I was invited to the school's graduation ceremony, where I would walk across the stage and receive my diploma. Dean asked Helga to my ceremony so she could see firsthand what I had accomplished all on my own and that I had proven her wrong.

"Will my sister be there?" Helga sneered.

"Yes, Mother, she will be, and if you want to go, you will promise to be nice and not start anything," I warned her.

"I will say and do whatever I like to her. You are in no position to tell me what to do!" Helga shouted.

"Well then, don't bother showing up to my graduation," I started, and I hung up the phone.

When the graduation ceremony day had finally come, I was nervous but excited at the same time. The day I had planned so long ago was finally here. I may have reached this point of my life not in the way I pictured it, but the fact was that this life was so much better than I could ever imagine. I missed soccer and hanging with my friends, but I was a wife and a mother, and those roles were so much more fulfilling. I arrived at the location of the ceremony, and I put on my grown, ready to have the two-hour event to begin. I had only been away from Dean and Elizabeth for an hour, but I missed them like crazy already. I took my seat and looked around at the auditorium; the graduates were all on the floor, and there were about three hundred of us all from different work-at-your-own pace schools. Up above us was a large balcony where our guests would be seated, and I was only expecting five people: my aunt Cathy and my uncle Simon, Dean, Elizabeth, and my papa. As I gazed around, I hadn't noticed who took the seat next to me.

"Well, fine, don't say hello." I turned to see that it was Seth.

"Hello, Seth," I laughed as I saw he was giving me his best diva look.

"Weren't you getting fat the last time I saw you?" he asked.

"I was incredibly huge until about two months ago when I lost a lot of weight. That's what happens when you have a baby," I told him.

"Well, you don't look like someone who just had a kid," Seth commented.

"Well, thank you, and I'm glad to see you finished this year. Also, I love the bright pink hair," I said, and before we could continue our conversation, the ceremony had started.

About forty minutes in, they had finally reached the *H*s. "Hailey Heart," the man on stage called out. I stood up and walked toward the steps that were connected to the side of the stage. I stopped and shook hands with my old principle, Mrs. Barton.

"Hailey, it's good to see you here," she commented as she shook my hand.

"Nothing was going to stop me from coming here today, not you and not my fellow students. Now I can show my daughter that nothing can stop you when you put your mind to something," I responded, and I left her on the note.

As I started to make my way across the stage, cheers began to go, and I was amazed at how many cheers I heard because I was expecting only a few people. I looked up into the crowd and was surprised to see a group of our friends along with my family had come out to see me graduate. The cheers continued as I walked up and received my diploma. I flipped the tassel on my cap to the other side and walked off the stage, and then the cheers finally died down.

When the ceremony was finally over, I said good-bye to Seth and sprinted to the outside courtyard so I could find everyone. I walked up to the group and received flowers and hugs, and after a few photos, I finally got my hands on Dean and Elizabeth. I was giving Elizabeth a ton of kisses when I saw something out of the corner of my eye. I turned to see the girls who had started the rumors about me at school. They were staring at me with what look like disbelief, but I didn't care. I turned away and followed my family to the parking lot.

Before I knew it, time flew by, and it had been a year and a half since my graduation, and things were better than ever. They were so good in fact that Dean and I decided that Elizabeth needed a little brother or sister. Soon after making that decision, it didn't take long for us to find out that I was pregnant with our second child. This time my pregnancy seemed to go by fast. I think it was because we knew what to expect, and we were much more prepared for this child than we were the first one. Or so we thought.

Our first sonogram was at three months, and we didn't really get to see much of the baby, but we do get to make sure the baby has a good heartbeat, and that's good enough for me. We got a clean bill of health, and we were told that our next sonogram was at six months, and at that appointment, we would find out the sex of the baby, so when the day finally came, we were excited just like a kid at Christmas. We went through the same routine with this appointment as we did at Elizabeth's sixth-month appointment, except we wouldn't be getting the same joyful news.

I knew something was wrong when fifteen minutes into the sonogram, Dr. Grey's face fell.

"Is there something wrong, Doctor?" I asked, and at the same time, Dean grabbed my hand, and I knew he saw the same sadness on the doctor's face as I did.

"I'm not sure yet. Give me a few more minutes… " Dr. Grey trailed off.

Out of all the times in my life that I thought the minutes had ticked by slow forever, this was so much worse than all those other times.

"Hailey, Dean, I am so sorry to be the one that has to tell you this… but… it seems your baby has some major problems," Dr. Grey informed.

"What kind of problems?" Dean asked because I was too shocked to get even a word out.

"Well, I can tell you what I see, but we won't have an exact diagnosis until I refer you to a specialist," Dr. Grey offered, and I looked toward her face, and I could see tears in her eyes.

"Okay, Doctor, what do you see?" I asked her. "Well, from the looks of it, the baby has spina bifida up to its neck, so it could be paralyzed from the waist down. Also, the baby seems to have a hole in one of the arteries in its heart, so right after the baby is born, it is going to need surgery to fix that, and the spine, if the baby's nerves in its back are exposed. There is also a massive amount of fluid on the baby's brain, which will require a stent, and the last thing I see is that the baby has clubbed hands and feet," Dr. Grey informed, and I couldn't believe my ears. Our poor baby had so many problems and so many challenges to overcome.

Before we left, Dr. Grey pulled me aside to talk to me. "I am so sorry about the news I had to give you," Dr. Grey apologized.

"It's okay. It's your job. I won't hold it against you," I muttered.

"There are times like this and cases like yours that I wish it wasn't my job," she stated. "Would you like to know the sex of your baby?" Dr. Grey asked.

"Yes, please," stammered Dean, and I just nodded my head.

"You're having a baby boy," she informed us, and I couldn't stop the tears as they followed down my face.

Dr. Grey referred us to a specialist by the name of Dr. Mark Matthews; unfortunately, we had to wait two days to see him. Dr. Grey gave us some printout pictures of our son, and she promised to keep in touch with us to look at how we are doing and said that if we ever need anything, we'd let her know.

We decided to go to our families with what we found out today, and everyone took it their own way. Kyle didn't say anything, and that's because I knew he didn't know what to say, and inside he was hurting too. Even though it was our son, it was his nephew. Donovan said he was sorry, and he would do anything to help. Charlie and Constantine took it hard, and they both cried. Mable and Julian gave their condolences, and they checked in every day for three days.

In those three days, I only made one mistake, and I chalked that up to grief. I went to my mother to tell her the news. I honestly didn't know what to expect. I didn't know if it was a mother's love or maybe something as simple as a hug and maybe "I'm sorry," but I definitely was not expecting what I got.

Dean and I arrived at Helga's house, which was located in a rural area, and it seemed like a friendly apartment complex. I knocked on the door, and a few seconds later, Helga answered, but I could tell that it had been a mistake to come here.

"What do you want?" she asked, not bothering to hide the hatred in her tone.

"We came here to share the news we have about your grandson," I answered, matching her tone while sliding my hand protectively over my belly.

"Fine. Come in," Helga stated as she let us inside. Once we were all inside and the door was closed, I started to explain because I wanted to get it over with as soon as possible. I explained to Helga what happened and what information we had, and then I handed her the pictures of the baby.

"What am I looking at?" she asked.

I moved closer and pointed out his problems and his clubbed hands and feet. That's when I saw her expression change from confusion to disgust.

She quickly shoved the photos back at me, and all she said was, "Oh... "

I became enraged, and I knew my face turned beat red as I started to yell, "*Oh*? That's it? *Oh*? I'm your daughter, and my heart is breaking I'm having your grandson and he isn't going to be able to be like other kids, and all you can say to me is *oh*!"

"What else should I say? I mean look at him. I will be more than happy to spend time with Elizabeth, but I just can't do it with your son," she stated as if it made common sense.

I took a deep breath and shuddered as my lungs gasped for the air. "Fuck you!" I said, and then I left slamming the door on my way out.

I shouldn't have been surprised. I know the type of person my mother was, but I thought that if it were her grandchild, she would change. Again, I shouldn't be surprised, especially considering that I once had a brother who had special needs. His name was William, and he was my best friend. He was so smart, knew every fact there was to know about Willey Nelson, and knew all his songs. He could also look at a picture and draw almost an exact copy on a blank piece of paper. Even though we had different mothers, where he was, I was, and I protected him in any way I could. However, when he turned twenty-one, my mother decided he was becoming too much to handle and stuck him in the first group home that would take him. She didn't even bother to run a background check, didn't care if he would be properly taken care of. Then one day, he was murdered. I later found out what happened. It seemed that the woman taking care of my brother also had her wheel chair–bound father living with her. Her dad one day accidently ran over the dog dish, spilling water all over the tile floor. In walked my shoeless and sockless brother, who slipped and fell, hitting the edge of a counter, causing the base of his spine to detach from the base of his brain. He would have lived had the woman taken him in; he would have surely been paralyzed, but he would have been alive. Instead, she shoved pain pills down William's throat and only finally called the paramedics when he started coughing up blood. Helga blamed me of course, said I didn't like him and that's why she sent him away. I thought that maybe she was saying this because she felt guilty, but all thoughts of that flew out the window when I found out my mother was suing the woman. She wasn't suing to have the woman's licenses taken away; she was suing for money, ten grand to be exact. She never spoke of him, and even though I still celebrated his birthday, no one else did.

When Dean and I were in the car, he pulled me close so he could hug me. "I'm sorry, sweetie," he soothed.

"I'm okay. I am not surprised, and I don't know why I thought this would change her. Let's just go," I said, and even though what my mom said hurt, I didn't feel the ache in my heart like I used to. Maybe my heart was so broken nothing could hurt it anymore.

Eventually, the day that we had scheduled with Dr. Matthews had finally come. We were nervous and devastated to be going, but we wanted to get more information about the condition of the baby. Thankfully, Dr. Matthews's office wasn't too far of a drive, and his testing office was located right next to the hospital where we had Elizabeth. As we pulled up to the building, I was surprised to see how dull the outside of the building looked. It was a crème-brown color, and it had no fancy big sign that announced that it was a doctor's office; it was just a building with a number on it. The only thing that told us that we were in the right place was from the tiny stenciled writing on the door that read "Dr. Mark Matthews."

The inside was entirely different. It looked just like any other doctor's office, full of chairs, quiet stillness, with lots of people. That's when I felt my heart break even more. In this tiny office, there were five other couples with tears in their eyes, and I knew that this was the place people came to when they were about to hear the worst news they could ever imagine.

The door made a loud slamming noise as it closed behind us, and I saw multiple sets of eyes look up at us. My heart nearly stopped in my chest when I saw the desperation, the sadness in their broad scared, sad eyes. I could see each and every one of their hearts breaking. I felt sorry for these parents and their babies because some of them might never get to meet their child, and most of these babies were likely to live a life full of pain, just like our son was destined to. We signed in at the receptionist's station and took our seats at the back of the room.

Our wait was only twenty minutes long; each one tick by was slow agony, but then they led us to a large room surrounded by machines and cabinets. I put on a gown that the nurse had given me, and I lay on the bed in the middle of the large room. Right as I was finished getting comfortable on the table, there was a knock on the door.

"Come in," I called.

"Hello, my name is Dr. Matthews," said the doctor politely.

Dean and I returned the introductions as we shook his hand.

"It's a pleasure to meet you. I wish it were under better circumstances," Dr. Matthews replied.

"Me too," I replied. My voice was shaking. All I wanted was to get more information about the baby.

"Well, let's get started. I know no form of bedside manner is going to ease your nervousness. So let's see what we can do to help your baby," Dr. Matthews comforted.

The first test was very simple and straightforward. Dr. Matthews took blood and did his own sonogram. It was the last test that terrified me. It was called an amniotic fluid test, also known as amniocentesis, and this test is done by inserting a large thin needle into the womb through my abdomen. They do this so they can draw out a little amniotic fluid so it can be tested to detect what kind of chromosomal abnormalities the baby might have. I didn't want a big needle anywhere near the baby, but Dr. Matthews promised me it was a safe procedure.

"Well, it is going to take us a day to analyze the fluid, so tomorrow I'd like you to come in and speak with our chromosome specialist, and I will have the test results by then. Also, before you go, here are some sono pictures for you, and I don't know if you knew already, but you're having a boy," Dr. Matthews whispered.

I didn't break down until I was in the car, and I cried the hardest I've ever cried until I was hiccupping. I thought that the safest place for my baby was in the womb. I never thought it could be his death bed.

CHAPTER 13

Sleeping Angel

It has been said time heals all wounds. I do not agree. The wounds remain. In time, the mind protecting its sanity covers them with scar tissue and the pain lessens, but it's never gone.
—Rose Kennedy

The next day, I couldn't get to Dr. Matthews office fast enough. Last night, I realized that I wasn't going to give up on our son. I would fight and protect him until the end. Dean and I also had agreed that no matter what was wrong with our little boy, we would love and take care of him for the rest of our lives.

Once we signed in, we were immediately taken to the back and to a row of offices until we reached the one that read "Dr. Miranda Lane, Chromosome Specialist." We entered the room and were instantly greeted by a woman. She was about five feet three inches, with a medium built, but her most noticeable feature was her bright red hair.

"Hello, my name is Miranda Lane. It's a pleasure to meet you. Please take a seat, and we will begin," she stated.

Dean and I sat together on a beige leather couch as Dr. Lane went toward a desk and retrieved a file folder.

"So your results are in, and before I explain them, I want to ask if it's okay I discuss them with you," Dr. Lane asked. "I know this might sound like an odd question, but seeing as I am not your doctor, this information is private. I can only look at it with your expressed consent," she explained.

"Yes, that's fine as long as our questions are answered," replied Dean.

"Yes, of course. So I'll get right to it. Your son does indeed have a chromosome abnormality. The type of abnormality he has is called trisomy 18 or Edward's syndrome," Dr. Lane started to explain.

"Are there different chromosome abnormalities that are categorized into different types?" I asked because I wondered which type was worse and if the baby had one of them.

"Yes, we categorize them mostly by severity along with other things. Your son has a condition that is caused by an error in cell division. Trisomy 18 occurs in about 1 out of every 2,500 pregnancies. Unfortunately, there's nothing you can do to prevent it, and with how young you both are, we believe this was a fluke. I say this because I know you both must be wondering if it's your fault and if you do decide to have more kids would it happen again," Dr. Lane explained.

"Yes, those were some of the things we were worried about. What are his chances of survival?" I asked, struggling to get the question said aloud. Was I going to receive an answer I didn't want to hear?

"This is always a hard question for me to answer. In these chromosome cases, most babies are lost in the second or third trimester as stillborn. There is only about 1 in 6,000 children that occur in living births," Dr. Lane whispered, and I knew she was telling us in the gentlest way possible.

"What are the chances of our baby being that 1 in 6,000?" I asked, my voice cracking.

"Your son has a lot of medical problems that we can see from the ultrasounds. He has severe spina bifida that reaches his neck, so when he is born, he will need surgery for that. He also has a hole in his heart that he will need surgery to repair. He has clubbed hands and feet and will most likely never have the use of either his hands or feet. The last thing we see is a large amount of fluid in his brain, and he will need a stent placed there to drain the liquid, so the odds are against him," Dr. Lane explained.

"Is he in pain?" I asked but was finally starting to cry.

"Right now, no, he is completely safe inside your womb, but I won't lie to you, when he is born, he is looking at a life filled with pain," Dr. Lane explained.

That's when I lost whatever little barrier I had left, and I felt an enormous tear in my heart. Dean asked some more questions that I couldn't hear because all I could do was cry.

Dr. Matthews joined us in the office right before we were about to leave. "Sorry for being late. It's been a crazy day," Dr. Matthews apologized.

"You're right on time, Mark. I answered the questions they had for me, so next is what questions they might have for you," Dr. Lane explained.

"I only have one question," I finally spoke up. "Will you be there for the delivery?" I asked Dr. Matthews.

"Yes, I will be there for both of you every step of the way," Dr. Matthews reassured. I felt a little comfort hearing that, but deep down, I knew the worst was yet to come.

After that, the days all seemed to roll into one as Dean and I prepared to take care of a baby that was going to have a lot of individual needs. We looked at equipment, beds, and communication items. Dean's family all pitched in to raise money for the baby; it wasn't a lot, but it was enough to pay bills and get some things we would need. We even picked out a name for the baby; we chose Keith Jacob Heart.

Today, Dean and I went about our day just like any other day. The only difference was that today's date was June 13, one of the many dates I'll never be able to forget.

Today both Dean and I had the day off, and neither of us felt like doing anything but staying inside all day. Since receiving the news about Keith, this was starting to become a constant thing for us. We were over at his mom's house watching TV when I felt a sudden pressure, and it felt like I had to pee. I quickly rushed to the bathroom. The bright light in the bathroom made me wince, so I had to squint and wait for my eyes to adjust to the change of light. Even though it was in the middle of the day, Dean had pulled the blinds closed in the room, so I've been in the dark all day. I sat on the toilet and was waiting to go when the sharp pressure came back, but this time more intense. Before I could grasp what was happening, the pressure came again, and then there was a sudden burst of liquid that came from between my legs. Panic shot through me as I realized that the liquid wasn't pee.

"*Dean!*" I screamed out as my panic became worse.

Dean was in the bathroom within seconds. "What happened?" he asked as he looked me over.

"I think my water broke," I exclaimed. Tears started to trek down my face.

"Isn't it too soon for that to happen?" Dean asked, and I could see the sadness fill his eyes. I couldn't even answer, so I shook my head. Dean ran out of the room, and I could hear him talking to his mom, telling her he was going to take me in. He came back into the bathroom and gently pulled me up off the toilet. After securing my sweats into place, he scooped me up and ran outside. He sat me down in the car and buckled me in before racing around to the driver's side and starting the car.

"What about Elizabeth?" I asked as Dean slipped into the driver side next to me.

"My mom said she would watch her," Dean replied as he started the car.

We arrived at the hospital sooner than I thought was possible, and I know that Dean chose to drive instead of waiting for an ambulance because time was significant. Before I could even get out of the car, Dean had me out and in his arms. "I've got you, baby. Everything is going to be okay," he reassured. As soon as we entered the front of the emergency area, Dean started yelling for help. "Somebody help us please!"

Automatically a nurse rushed out towards us. "What's going on?" she asked while checking me over.

"My wife... her water broke... " Dean explained, breathing heavily.

"Someone get me a wheelchair," the nurse called to the back. "How far along is she?"

"About six months," Dean choked.

Everything after that moment was a blur. Dr. Matthews arrived and confirmed that my water had indeed broken. Dean was pacing back and forth as Dr. Matthews was checking a few more things.

"Dr. Matthews, I'm sorry to disturb you, but I want to see if you wanted a swab to take samples," the nurse asked Dr. Matthews.

"No, there's no need for that. If you could please give me a moment with Mr. and Mrs. Heart," Dr. Matthews asked politely. As soon as the nurse left the room, Dr. Matthews addressed us. "I have some awful news... Your baby doesn't have a heartbeat," Dr. Matthews stated sadly.

I couldn't believe my ears. Keith didn't have a heartbeat? Our baby was dead?

Dr. Matthews explained to us what would happen next, but I couldn't stop shaking or crying long enough to ask any questions. My baby was gone. I'd never feed him, I would never see him grow, and I wouldn't be able to hold him and kiss him every day. My heart shattered into a million pieces, and I didn't know if it would ever be able to be put back together again.

A special room was set up for us upstairs, and Dean carried me up to the room, refusing to let the nurses take me in a hospital bed. By this time, I had run out of tears and was now in complete shock. I didn't know what to do or how to think. My head was full of my chaotic emotions, and my chest hurt to the point where I felt like I was dying.

"I am so sorry, baby," Dean whispered as he gently placed me in the bed in our private room.

"He's gone, Dean. Our baby is gone," I cried, and that's all I could do.

Eventually, Dr. Matthews and a nurse came to start the inducement process. It seems that even though my water broke, my labor was at a standstill. I was now at a high risk of getting an infection.

The first thing Dr. Matthews did was use a gel to strip the membranes in the walls of my uterus. This was supposed to help begin the labor process. After six hours of labor, I only dilated half a centimeter.

Once Dr. Matthews realized that this was not working, he went on to inject me with a hormone that was supposed to open my cervix and trigger contractions. After eight hours of contractions, I was only two centimeters dilated.

"Hailey, please let me give you something for the pain. I know you must be in a lot of pain," Dr. Matthews sympathetically asked.

It was true. I was in a great deal of pain, but I would suffer through. *This is what I deserve,* I thought. "I'm all right, Doctor, but thank you," I replied as I rode on the next wave of contractions.

Once Dr. Matthews decided I wasn't dilating fast enough, he went on to try something else. I was then given another medication through my IV. This medication was to be given to me a little at first then more and more in order to make my contractions consistent and active in order to help me give birth to Keith.

Ten hours later and well into day two of labor, I was only three centimeters dilated. I could see the sorrow in Dr. Matthews's eyes as he watched me, knowing I was suffering but not able to do anything about it. As more and more hours passed, with still no progress, Dr. Matthews made one last decision to keep rotating through the inducement procedures until I finally became fully dilated.

Dean's sister Alice decided to take Elizabeth to Phoenix where she lived in order to give Dean and I the time we needed to deal with what was going on. I didn't want to have someone else take care of Elizabeth, but I couldn't take care of her like she needs right now, and I don't want her to see what was going on. So I kissed her good-bye and went back to controlling the waves of contractions.

It had been almost four days since we arrived at the hospital. Four days since we lost our baby boy and four days of trying to hold ourselves together. Dean and I have a great support team. Constantine never left our side, and she always made sure we ate. She tried to get me to talk more. She brought us movies, drinks, and comfort. The only time she left was when she went home to sleep.

Simone was also there. She was kind, supportive, and did everything she could to be there. She slept in a chair in the corner of the room and only left to get food.

"Hey," Simone whispered to me one night, and I turned in my bed to look at her. "I know nothing I say can make this better, but know we are family, always have been, and I will always be here for you," she commented.

Tears sprung to my eyes. "Thank you, Simone," and then I wept silently.

"Hey, baby, you okay?" Dean asked as he came and stood next to me.

"No," I whispered as I tried and failed at holding back my sobs.

"Oh, love, I'm so sorry," Dean croaked, tears filling his eyes. He moved around the bed and moved the rail down from the side of my bed.

"Can you move over, baby?" Dean asked, and I knew he didn't want me to hurt myself. I scooted over, and as soon as I did, he climbed into the bed next to me. "Talk to me, baby. Don't shut me out. I am still here with you, my love, all the way," Dean coaxed.

"I am so sorry I couldn't keep our baby safe, Dean," I cried as I turned to Dean's chest.

"You heard the doctors. There was nothing, *nothing*, we could do. You gave our child a loving environment of comfort and peace for six months. I would give anything to have Keith back, but he died in peace. He didn't know pain, all he knew was love, your love… our love," Dean insisted. Then he kissed me with an earth-shattering kiss, and I didn't deserve to feel bliss, but I couldn't help it. Dean held me the rest of the night and massaged my lower back as I rolled through the contractions.

It was nighttime on the fourth night when I had finally become dilated enough to be able to start pushing.

"Okay, Hailey, this is what we have been waiting for. Dr. Matthews is on his way, but we need you to start pushing now," Nurse Beth stated.

"I am supposed to deliver with no doctor?" I panted. My body began to shake from both nerves and devastation.

"No, there is a doctor coming up here right now. He will stand in the place of Dr. Matthews until he gets here," the nurse reassured.

As if called on cue, Dr. Matthews's replacement came in. "Hello, Mr. and Mrs. Heart, I am Dr. Zane. I will be stepping in until Dr. Matthews gets here," the new doctor explained coldly.

He quickly donned gloves and checked my progress, with no more words exchanged. After a few minutes, he finally spoke, "Well,

Dr. Matthews may not make it in time. It is time to push, Mrs. Heart," he stated.

Even though I desperately wanted to wait for Dr. Matthews, I couldn't stop myself from pushing. It took all my strength, all my love, all my pain, and all my sadness. And I pushed. Three pushes later, and I knew Keith was out. The silence that followed shattered my heart, the heart that had slowly been pieced together by Dean and his love was now fragmented into thousands of pieces.

What happened next broke me even more.

I sat up in my bed and extended my hands so I could hold my baby. It didn't matter if he was born dead or what he looked like; he was my little boy, and I wanted to hold him. Instead of being given my son, I watched in horror as Dr. Zane took our little boy's lifeless body and discarded him into a hazard waste bin. I was frozen in place by shock, and a little whimper fell from my lips. I heard a growl come from Dean, and I looked at him in time to see him take off toward the doctor.

The next sound that was heard was the loud crack of someone being smacked. My gaze turned toward the sound, and instead of seeing Dean in a fight, I looked on as my nurse lowered her hand after having smacked Dr. Zane.

"*How dare you do that?*" she screamed before turning around and scooping my son out of the bin. "I'm going to clean him up and bring him to you," she said addressing me.

By this time, Dean and Dr. Zane were in a yelling match when a voice boomed out, "*What is going on here?*" Dr. Matthews yelled.

"Dr. Zane here threw this innocent child in the hazard waste bin," Nurse Beth explained.

Dr. Matthews stiffened as he turned himself toward his fellow doctor. "What were you thinking? How could you do something like that?"

"Well… I couldn't stand to look at him," Dr. Zane replied.

"Are you serious?" Dr. Matthews yelled. "You work for me and my practice. We specialize in high-risk pregnancies. You will see this a lot. You're fired," Dr. Matthews stated.

"What?" Dr. Zane gasped.

"You heard me. You are fired. You apparently cannot handle this line of work. I do not want someone like you associated with this practice. Don't bother using me as a reference for your next job either. I will paint you like the heartless person you are." And with that final statement, he opened the door, letting Dr. Zane out of the room.

"Dean, Hailey, I am so sorry. You shouldn't have had to deal with that on top of everything else," Dr. Matthews stated before stepping back and allowing Nurse Beth to bring Keith to me.

"Here is your beautiful baby boy," she whispered.

I could see that she had cleaned the blood and gunk off of Keith. He was also swaddled in a tiny blanket. It was the one we bought him after we found out we were having a boy.

"Would you like to hold him?" Beth was asking before handing us our son.

"Yes," I croaked out.

She turned toward the small hospital crib in the corner and gathered the tiny bundle in her arms. As she grew closer, I could see how small he was.

"Here's your little angel," Beth murmured.

She handed over the tiny bundle, and I couldn't believe how tiny he was. He was so much smaller than I first realized I was able to hold him with one hand.

One by one, those who had stayed with us for the past four days came over to say good-bye to Keith.

Constantine came to us first, and her gaze roamed over Keith. I could see the tears that began to gather at the corner of her eyes. "He looks so much like Dean," she commented.

Everyone else took their turn, and then Dean and I were alone in the room, and that is all it took for me to break down. I cried harder than I ever had in my entire life.

"Shh, baby, let it out. I am sorry, so sorry," Dean repeated over and over until my tears ran dry. He held us both until I finally stopped spilling tears, and he looked at me as I hiccupped, gasped for air, and tried to talk.

"I want our baby back, and I want to feel him warm in my arms. I want to see him grow up and fall in love. I want him back," I chanted over and over.

"I know, baby, but he is in a better place. He is pain-free, in heaven, with all of our loved ones. I know that he is going to be our little angel and be watching over all of us," Dean soothed.

I knew he was right, but all I could do was cry, feeling shattered, broken, and robbed.

"He is so beautiful," I cried.

Shortly after, a priest came in to baptize Keith.

"My child, I want you to know that even though he passed away before he was baptized, the Lord has still accepted him into his arms," the priest reassured.

CHAPTER 14

Pain

Once you had put the pieces back together, even though you may look intact, you were never quite the same as you'd been before the fall.
—Jodi Picoult

I was released from the hospital a day later, with no baby and in more pain than I could imagine. The doctor prescribed me pain medicine, but I refused to take it. I deserved this pain. I couldn't keep my baby safe.

That day, we left to go get Elizabeth, and I couldn't wait to get her in my arms.

When we finally reached her in Phoenix, it comforted me to see how happy she was, and I was glad she wasn't anywhere near us when Dean and I were in the hospital.

"Mommy! Daddy!" Elizabeth shouted as she ran toward us. I gathered her close and whispered to her how much I loved her and how I promised always to protect her.

Two weeks later.

No parent should ever bury their child. No parent should ever have to go through what Dean and I were experiencing. Dean's family was very supportive during this time, and they even helped to fundraise money for Keith's funeral expenses, so we had less to worry about. My aunt Cathy and Papa helped in so many amazing ways and gave us the rest of the money needed to put Keith to rest.

Before I knew it, it was the day of Keith's memorial service. Several friends and family showed up. It made me happy, knowing that even though no one met him, he had so many people who loved him.

I was offered apologies and condolences. Some people asked how I was feeling and tried to add some form of positive thought into the tragic event we went though. Many said they were comforted knowing that he passed away safely in my womb without knowing any pain, and in that aspect, I had to agree with them. From what the doctor told me, after Keith was born, he would've needed three surgeries, and he would need to have more surgeries continually as he grew. It would be a painful life. Even though, I wanted my son alive more than anything else in the world, I took small comfort in knowing he was pain-free.

People took turns talking. A lot of our friends talked about our relationship and how they knew that together we would move on. Next, Dean's father, Charlie, decided to share a story.

"I haven't told anyone but Constantine this story yet because I felt that it would be better if I shared it today," Charlie explained. "Keith saved my life the other day," Charlie stated, and a collective gasp went through the crowd. "Many of you guys today received rubber bracelets in memory of Keith. Well, we have had them for a couple days now. Anyway, the other day, I was at work, and for those who may not know what I do, I work with motors," Charlie continued. "This day I was working on a motor in the shop. Everything was going the way it always does until I asked one of the guys to shut the motor off so I could take a look at it on the inside. I was told it was off, so I reached my hand inside. However, it was still live. There are thousands and thousands of volts of electricity running through one of these motors. Touching it while it is on can stop your heart and kill you. My Keith bracelet had touched the machine before I did, and because it was rubber, it acted as a barrier and informed me of the still-active motor. So my grandson Keith saved my life." Charlie finished and walked up to hug me as the tears rolled down my checks. The moment however did not last long because it was interrupted by the doorbell ringing.

I wiped the tears falling from my eyes as I made my way to the front door. I should have never opened it.

Standing there was the one person I never wanted to see again, especially not at my baby's memorial service.

"What the hell are you doing here?" I hissed at Helga.

"I was invited, and I also have every right to be here," she seethed back.

"Who would ever invite you?" I asked, angered.

Helga opened her mouth to answer, but before she could someone else answered.

"I invited her."

I quickly turned around and saw that Constantine was the one who answered.

"What? Why? You know how I feel about her and what she has done to me and those I love. She didn't even care about him when I went and saw her!" I shouted.

"I understand, Hailey, but she is technically his grandmother. I also never want you to regret her not coming. It is her only chance to say good-bye. Do it for your son," Constantine soothed.

I didn't agree with her, but I knew that she might be in some way correct. I turned towards my mother and gave her a warning I knew I would never regret. "You can come in, but I swear to God if you in anyway ruin today or are mean to those I love, you will regret it."

I walked back into the main room, and Dean took one look and knew what was wrong.

"Where is she?" he asked.

"Headed this way. Your mom invited her."

"What?" he asked, and I saw the shock on his face.

"It's okay, baby. She did what she thought was right, and I already warned Helga to watch her behavior," I said as I grabbed his hand and led him back toward our friends and family.

Everything was fine for a while, but then everything fell down like blocks in a tower. Surprising, it did not start with my mother. Dean and I had sent out invitations to Keith's memorial service to friends and family on Facebook. The main picture for the event and my profile picture was of Keith.

It was thanks to the nurses that I had a picture of him at all. After cleaning Keith off, the nurses then dressed him in a tiny outfit and took some very sweet, cute pictures of him. I was so grateful to them for this amazing cherished gift. However, not everyone shared my opinion. During Keith's memorial service, I received a private message from two of my friends on Facebook.

"We wanted to ask you to please remove this photo from Facebook."

I couldn't believe what I had just read.

"How could you ask me to do this?" I replied to the people I considered friends, one I even considered a best friend.

"It's just that it is a hard picture to look at," they wrote.

"Then do not look at him," I shouted through the message.

"If you do not remove it, we will report it to Facebook. We just feel that his picture should be only kept at home and placed on the back of the bookshelf," they replied with ease.

I was so furious I was shaking. I had nothing left to say to these girls I once considered friends. So I removed them from my account and vowed never to speak to them again. Everyone has the right to his or her opinions, but no one will ever tell me that I should be embarrassed of my son.

I later found out that they did report my son's photo to Facebook, who asked me to remove it. I explained to them that they were wasting their time and that if others could have naked chicks and gang signs as their profile picture, then I could have my picture of my beautiful son. If they tried to remove it themselves, then I would see them in court.

The day only got worse from there and that I could thank my mother for. After what I just went through, Dean and I were in sour moods. It was at that moment that I overheard Helga talking to others about being a grieving grandmother.

"Mother, please don't... don't act like you lost something dear to you. When I went to you, you told me straight to my face that you would be a grandmother to Elizabeth but not to Keith," I interrupted. I wasn't trying to out her in front of everyone, but I was not going to let her get the attention she wants especially on today of all days.

My mother looked completely shocked, and her face turned red in anger. "I am very glad that Keith didn't live. You are in no way capable of taking care of a child with special needs. You would have eventually have left him on my front door step." She snickered.

"Get out of this house now!" I screamed, not caring if I made a scene. "I would never give up on my child, and I would especially never subject my child to the same childhood both me and my brother William went through."

She left, and I don't care whether she felt that she won. I knew that in the grand scheme of things she lost the most.

After she left, I said good-bye to three things that day: my past, my baby, and a part of my heart.

CHAPTER 15

The Rift

Nothing was okay anymore, and I couldn't seem to pull myself out of the darkness that was trying to swallow me alive. There was this ever-growing rift between Dean and me. There was no more happiness, and I know we both blame ourselves. The only time we smile anymore was around Elizabeth, but seeing her sometimes made me want to cry. I looked at her and saw one beautiful healthy child when I should have two. Dean tried to talk to me, and I didn't want to push him away, but I always seemed to do just that. I know that I would lose him too; it was only a matter of time.

"Okay, enough!" Dean shouted as he stormed his way into our bedroom. I flew back, shocked because I had never heard him used this tone before. "We are talking now! I feel you slipping away from me, and I cannot lose you too!" Dean continued.

"What is there to say? Our baby is gone. I couldn't protect him. We won't see him grow up, won't hear his laugh, or know his voice, and it is all my fault," I spat as the tears poured down my face once more.

"That's what you truly thinking? That this is your fault?" he asked, the tone of disbelief in his voice.

All I could do is nodded my head yes.

"Baby, it was his chromosomes that took him from us. You have no control over that," Dean whispered sitting himself on the edge of the bed.

"I understand that, but I still feel the way I do," I sobbed. "I can feel us drifting too, and I know you are going to leave me. I don't blame you. I can't even look at myself in the mirror," I continued.

"Enough! I never want to hear you say that again. I am never going anywhere. It has always been you. Don't you understand that?" Dean shouted again.

"What are you talking about?" I asked, confused by the look of determination on his face.

"I loved you from the first moment I saw you!" Dean stated seriously.

"At Simone's party, I know, I felt the same—"

"No," Dean said, cutting me off. "Long before then," he whispered, releasing a secret I felt he hadn't told anyone.

"What are you talking about?" I asked, confused, and it was then that my heart kick-started back to life and started fluttering again like it used to whenever he was near.

"The first time I ever saw you was one night when I walked a female coworker home because I didn't want her to walk alone in the middle of the night. There you were, staring out of the window of an apartment, staring at me through these big-framed glasses. I wanted to so badly go and talk to you, but I was sixteen and scared shitless because I never felt in my entire life what I did for you when I first saw you."

I opened my mouth to try and say something, but he held up a finger, signaling he wasn't finished. "Your sister quit just a couple of days after that night, and I thought I had missed my chance. Until the day I start my new job at a video store, and there you were! Like God himself had smiled down on me. I knew I couldn't waste this opportunity, and I talked to you, and you were amazing! Smart, beautiful, and a dreamer, but I could just tell by talking to you that a boy like me and dating were the farthest thing from your mind. I thought it might be because you were younger than I had thought. You were tall, but you had this innocence that surrounded you, so I backed off. I hoped every day that I went to work that I would see you, and when I did, it would make my day. Then I didn't see you for weeks, and I knew I wouldn't anymore."

My mouth grew dry as I search my memories of the video store. I pulled up the image of the cute boy who worked behind the counter. Sure enough, I knew it was Dean, just a younger version. I was blown away when Dean continued, not believing there could possibly be more.

"Then there was one more time a few months before Simone's party where I saw you again. It was at the KFMAYDAY concert, and I was with Kyle and Simone, but you were with some of your other friends, and we all stood around talking, enjoying the music. I was in heaven being able to stand near you, and every fiber in my being screamed out to ask you out. Yet it wasn't the right time again. I had just started dating Nicole, and you were in your own world. Like this beautiful goddess I knew I could never touch. You stood there with your eyes closed, dancing to the music as it coursed through you, and I was in love forever. I knew, standing there and watching you, that you had stolen my heart."

Sobs waked my body, but this time in joy. Hearing how he felt and seeing myself through his eyes, I could never doubt anymore. Dean quickly came to me and wrapped me in his arms, and I felt whole once more. I would remain scared, but he helped in mending me.

Once I had calmed down, I was able to finally speak. "Why did you never tell me?"

"I was just waiting for the right time… " he whispered.

CHAPTER 16

Mended

And then the day came, when the risk to remain tight in a
bud was more painful than the risk it took to blossom.
—Anais Nin

Ten months later.

"It's time," I heard the doctor say, and my heart started beating in my chest.

"Where's my husband?" I asked, trying to not let my voice shake.

"He is on his way, Hailey. I need you to push," Dr. Matthews comforted.

"I am sorry, Doctor, but I am not pushing until he is here," I grunted as I gritted my teeth against the new wave of pain.

"I'm here!" shouted Dean from somewhere behind me.

"About time," I said, exhaling a sigh of relief, being so happy to see him.

"Sorry, they made me put on these scrubs before I could come into the OR," Dean explained as he came to my side and placed a quick kiss on my lips.

It had not been that long since Dean and I lost Keith, but to us it felt like a lifetime. After Keith passed away, it felt like we had begun to drift apart. Not knowing how to deal with the pain and our broken hearts, we turned away from each other instead of coming together to see each other out of the dark. As always, we found our way back to each other because we never have been able to stay apart. Dean helped to mend my broken heart. We didn't plan on getting pregnant again so soon, but when we found out, we believed it was what we needed.

Whenever we look at our beautiful daughter, we saw only one kid when in our hearts we knew there should have been two. We knew there was a chance that when we had this baby there would be the chance that we would feel like we should have three but we would only have two. However, we felt that God took care of that for us.

"Here comes the first baby, Hailey. I need you to push for me," Dr. Matthews coaxed.

I pushed as hard as I could, and in no time, I heard the best sound in the whole world: a brand-new baby was screaming.

"Here's your beautiful baby boy!" Dr. Matthews shouted. "He is healthy and has all ten fingers and toes," he commented as he held up the baby for us to see before passing him off to the nurse so she and the other doctor could do a checkup on him.

"Okay, Hailey, I know you have had only a few minutes of rest, but I need you to start pushing again," Dr. Matthews coaxed.

I repeated the earlier process and started to push down as hard as I could.

"Okay, Hailey, take a breather, and as soon as possible, I want you to push again."

"Come on, baby, one last big push. You can do it," Dean whispered and squeezed my hand.

A minute later, I was ready, and I started pushing again.

"That's it, Hailey. Almost there. Keep going," the doctor encouraged, and it was at that moment that I felt the pressure release from my stomach.

"We have baby boy number two!" Dr. Matthews exclaimed.

I did not hear the incredible sound of crying. "Why isn't he crying? Is he okay?" I panicked and looked to Dean for comfort.

"It's okay, Hailey. He is fine. Just be calm," Dr. Matthews reassured, and sure enough, after some encouraging on the doctor's part, I heard the loud wail of my newborn son.

The doctor showed us the baby and then joined the staff in the back of the room to evaluate the other baby, leaving Dean and me alone.

"You are so amazing, baby," Dean stated as he continued to kiss me all over my face.

"Where's Cathy?" I asked, noticing now that Dean had come in alone.

"Sorry, sweetie, they said only one could come in, and she insisted it would be me," he explained.

"Of course it should be you. You're going to be a daddy again. You couldn't miss this. I wouldn't let you!" I exclaimed.

A lot had happened over the last ten months. My aunt became a large part of my family's life. She showed me what it truly meant to be a mother, and because I had always been close to her in my childhood, with her permission, I refer to her as Mom now, and Elizabeth knows her as Grandma.

When Dean and I found out we were pregnant, we were very shocked and scared. We received mixed reviews from people. Some thought it was too soon, and others were very happy for us. We were terrified of going through what we had gone through with Keith, but at our sixth-month appointment, instead of receiving bad news, we were told that not only were we having one healthy baby but two! I will never forget that moment for as long as I live because when Dean found out, he ran up and down the hallway with our two-year-old in tow, screaming, "We are having twins!"

"By the way, happy third-year anniversary," Dean said, snapping me out of my flashback before kissing me the way that still drives me crazy.

"That's right, it is April 21. You know that this means the twins have a birthday on our anniversary," I commented, and a huge smile covered my face.

"You should know by now, baby, that with us, everything comes full circle." Dean smiled.

After returning to my room, we were finally able to hold our babies. Looking upon the faces, I saw a little of Keith in both of them and felt my heart mend together once again.

My heart had been shattered, but thanks to Dean and the children he gave me, it was mended back together. The scars remain and will stay there forever as a road map of a story.

"Did you decide on their names?" the nurse asked us.

"Yes," we said in unison.

"The first boy we have named Jayden James Heart," I replied.

"The other twin will be called Kayden Jacob Heart," Dean added.

Elizabeth climbed onto the bed, giving me and the babies a gentle hug, and soon Dean joined in. Dean and I have overcome so much, and our love has only grown. He is my other half, the light to my darkness, and he will own my heart forever. We have overcome the obstacles thrown at us, and we have grown stronger, together. I know that whatever else we may be challenged with, we will overcome because in the end no matter what there is a mended heart beneath these scars.

Epilogue

Though no one can go back and make a brand-new start,
anyone can start from now and make a brand-new ending.
—Carl Bard

Four years later.

"Dean, hurry up, or we are going to be late," I called upstairs.

"I am coming. Had to grab the camera. Are the kids ready to go?"

"Yes. Elizabeth had been pacing nonstop. Let's go." I laughed.

We loaded up the kids into the car, and I couldn't help but feel the nervous knots in my stomach only get tighter. Today our baby girl was graduating kindergarten, and I couldn't believe how much time had already flown by. I looked over my shoulder into the back seat and gazed lovingly at our kids. Elizabeth was wearing a pink dress, living up to the Princess nickname I call her. Of course, her brothers wanted to dress up as well, so both of them were sporting dress pants with a dress shirt and vest. All our babies were so different with their own personalities, and I loved how unique they were. Elizabeth was outgoing and made friends wherever she went, and she was currently in love with art and was good at it too. Jayden was my tech-savvy boy because he loved anything to do with electronics and was getting very good at playing games with his daddy. Kayden was another story; he was more shy and sensitive. He was a total Momma's boy, but you would never hear me complain about it.

Every day I woke up more and more grateful than the day before. I had healthy, beautiful children, and the love of my life was the father of them. When the twins turned four, we celebrated not only their birthday but also our seventh-year wedding anniversary. It never seemed like that long, and I knew it never will because no amount of time will ever be long enough with Dean.

As we pulled up to the front of the school, Dean dropped off Elizabeth and me so I could take her to her graduating class while he looked for a parking spot. Walking toward Elizabeth's classroom, I couldn't help but think about how far I have come, how much I loved being a mother, and if I had to do it all over again, nothing would change. I would do everything again, the heartache, the pain, the joy, and the happiness. It all shaped me into who I have become, and I am someone I can be proud of. I have the guy of my dreams, my kids are happy and healthy, and they will never know the pain I did as a child. I have earned my associates degree in psychology and am attending again to earn my bachelor's degree. I am an aunt to so many wonderful nieces and nephews, fourteen of them to be exact. Dean gave me a family and so much happiness that my pain that resides in my past no longer hurts as much as it once did. The darkness that once showed its ugly head no longer exists, and even though I am covered in scars that only Dean and I can see, beneath them is a mended heart.

Soon after dropping Elizabeth off, we gathered with our other family and friends. Once everyone was in place, music started, and tears gathered in my eyes as I watched the joy on Elizabeth's face form as she started singing her graduation song. I felt a warm hand grab mine that soon led to sparks, and I knew without even looking that Dean was at my side.

"Look at the boys, baby," Dean whispered, and I glanced over to them to see them shaking their little butts to the beat of the song. I couldn't help but chuckle as happiness filled my heart.

The song soon came to an end, and the principal started calling out the names. When it was Elizabeth's turn, everyone hooted, hollered, and cheered. Since Keith, I have learned to cherish every single day because we never know when it may be our last.

Later that night, after getting the kids ready for bed, Dean stopped me and pushed me against the wall. "God, I love you so much. I grow more thankful for you every day. Have I told you today how happy you make me feel?" Dean whispered before leaning into me. He kissed me like he was starving. I arched my back, trying to always get closer to him. It wasn't until we finally separated that I was finally able to answer him.

"You only told me twice today," I replied, putting a fake pout on my face.

"How dare I slack in my duties," Dean replied, his mock horror being instantly replaced by his boyish smile. "You have made me the happiest man alive," he whispered and then kissed me again.

He pulled away quickly to swat me on the butt. "Now get in there and read our babies their bedtime story so I can finally have you to myself." Dean smirked.

Once I entered the twins' room, Elizabeth was already there, and I was greeted at all at once, "Mommy, is it story time?"

"Yes, it is," I chuckled my reply. "What will it be tonight?" I sat down on the edge of one of the beds.

"Tell us the story about you and Daddy," Elizabeth answered, and both Jayden and Kayden nodded their heads in agreement.

This was a story I found to be telling them more and more. I once explained to them that it was an old tale that reminded me of me and their father. Now they just thought it was about us, and I was okay with that because in many ways, I believed it was.

Everyone bunkered down as I started telling the story I have told nearly a hundred times now.

"According to the Greek mythology, humans were originally created with four arms, four legs, and a head with two faces. Fearing their power, Zeus sent down his thunderbolts, splitting them into two separate beings, condemning them to spend their lives in search of their other halves… and I found mine."

Some would call our story an epic love story, but we call it fate. All the choices we made led us to each other because every choice can change the future. If we had made the smallest different choice, it may have never been our time, but I would do everything all over again in a heartbeat.

Dean and Hailey's Playlist

Welcome to My Life - Simple Plan (Hailey's childhood)

Why Can't I - Liz Phair (When Hailey meets Dean)

Count on Me - Bruno Mars (Dean and Hailey's friendship)

Your Guardian Angel - The Red Jumpsuit Apparatus (Hailey's Myspace song to Dean)

Damn Regret - The Red Jumpsuit Apparatus (Dean's Myspace song to Hailey)

I'm Yours - Jason Mraz (Dean asking Hailey out)

Just a Kiss - Lady Antebellum (Dean and Hailey's start of the relationship)

Because of You - Kelly Clarkson (Hailey's song to her mom)

Bleeding Love - Leona Lewis (When Hailey met and fell in love with Dean)

She Is Love - Parachute (Dean's song about Hailey)

Iris - The Goo Goo Dolls (Hailey's song to Dean)

Beautiful with You – Halestorm (How Dean makes Hailey feel)

Two Is Better than One - Boys Like Girls feat. Taylor Swift (Dean and Hailey's song to each other)

Marry Me - Train (When Dean proposes)

Never Stop – Safetysuit (Dean and Hailey's wedding day)

Fall for You - Secondhand Serenade (They always come full circle)

I Won't Give Up - Jason Mraz (When they lost Keith)

Fix You - Coldplay (Dean and Hailey after losing Keith)

Hear You Me - JIMMY EAT WORLD (Keith's song)

The First Time Ever I Saw Your Face - Leona Lewis (How Hailey felt
    every time she gave birth to a child)
Wherever You Will Go - The Calling
Get around This - SafetySuit
Better than I Know Myself - Adam Lambert
Stolen - Dashboard Confessional
You Are the One - Shiny Toy Guns
Smother Me - The Used
Only One - Yellowcard
Love Song - The Cure
Everything - Lifehouse
Breathe – Angels and Airwaves
Just a Step Away - Carly Rae Jepsen
Heart - The Pretty Reckless
If I Didn't Have You - Thompson Square
Clarity - Zedd ft. Foxes
A Thousand Years Part 2 - Christina Perri ft. Steve Kazee
There for You - Flyleaf
Until the Day I Die - Story of the Year
With Me - Sum 41
Army – Ellie Goulding
Stand by You - Rachel Platten

Freedom

I can be whoever I want to be.
The choice is up to me.
I have hopes and I have dreams.
With those, you can't stop me,
So leave me alone.
Get out of my face.
I'm going to break free from this place.
And in the end you're going to see,
What exactly I make of me.

Forbidden Love

The hardest thing to do is to be next to someone you know you can
have.
Do I pretend these feelings don't exist?
I wonder why I am acting like this.
I'm losing my mind
Because I feel like I'm just wasting my time.
I can see it, when I get close,
That's when I need you the most.
My knees go weak
When you look at me.
These are the things I've never said,
And now I'll never know what could have been.
I'm stepping up
And letting everything out.
And I am going to jump and shout.
Just to show you that I like you a lot.

It's You

He asked, "Why me?"
And then suddenly, all the words came out like a symphony.
It's you, because no words can describe how I feel,
For it's you that leave me breathless.
It's you, because we were meant to be,
For it's our paths that are crossed endlessly.
It's you, because in your eyes I can see my life,
For it's you that have my heart.
It's you, because your touch liquefies me,
For it is your touch that sparks my desire.
It's you, because life without you is no life at all,
For it's you that fill the void in my heart.
It's you, because the sun will set and the moon will rise,
But I know it's you, because it hit me like a tide.
You came to me on Cupid's wings,
And it cannot hide that I didn't pick you,
It was you that picked me.

Goodnight,
My Sleeping Angel

Even though it was not meant to be,
I feel as though you were taken from me.
Not a day goes by
That I don't tell the lie
That my heart is just fine,
When really inside a part of me has died.
I only held you for a brief moment,
But I will carry you with me always.
I felt you move,
I felt you grow,
And then I felt you die.
And I know that I will never be all right.
You changed me.
You broke me.
I lost myself
The day I lost you.
I cried for you until I no longer felt.
I tried to hide from all the pain and suffering.
I didn't know how to cope,
I tried to sew my heart back,
But the emptiness still remains,
But the sadness never seems to go away.
My sleeping angel,
There's a missing piece.
That has been cast away…
On the day that you died…

The day my heart broke…
Life will never be complete without you.
Good night, my sleeping angel.
May my soul hold you tight.
Goodnight, my sleeping angel
Until the day I see you again
Until the day I get to hold you once again.
Goodnight, my sleeping angel.

About the Author

C. L. Harris lives in Tucson, Arizona, where she met her husband of eight years. Together they have a seven-year-old little girl and twin four-year-old boys. C. L. Harris wasn't raised in the idealistic American home and greatly struggled throughout her adolescence, often with depression and the tragic road that so often follows. She had met a young man who, through friendship, showed her that contrary to what she had been made to believe her whole life, she did have value and was perfectly unique just the way she was. C. L. Harris bore her soul in her debut novel, *A Mended Heart beneath These Scars* while the severity of most of these true events remains unwritten. It is her hope that she can reach young adults who have been in similar situations and give them a new sense of hope that no matter how hard things have been, the future is unwritten and there are many wonderful things waiting for them. All they need is hope and to love themselves as the beautiful and unique individuals that they are. C. L. Harris wants to encourage anyone who reads this novel not to give up on themselves because like the author, you too can achieve your dreams.

CPSIA information can be obtained
at www.ICGtesting.com
Printed in the USA
FSOW02n1658061016
25696FS

9 781633 383067